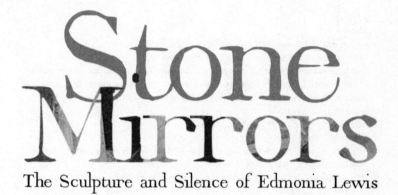

Stone Mirrors

The Sculpture and Silence of Edmonia Lewis

Jeannine Atkins

atheneum

Atheneum Books for Young Readers

New York   London   Toronto   Sydney   New Delhi

3 - 13 -17

Many thanks to Jane Harstad, D.Ed.,
a Mille Lacs Band descendant and a
member of the Red Cliff Band of Ojibwe,
for the thoughtful review.

A
atheneum

An imprint of Simon & Schuster Children's Publishing Division
1230 Avenue of the Americas, New York, New York 10020

Text copyright © 2017 by Jeannine Atkins
Jacket illustration copyright © 2017 by Ekua Holmes

For information about special discounts for bulk purchases, please contact Simon & Schuster Special Sales at 1-866-506-1949 or business@simonandschuster.com.
The Simon & Schuster Speakers Bureau can bring authors to your live event. For more information or to book an event, contact the Simon & Schuster Speakers Bureau at 1-866-248-3049 or visit our website at www.simonspeakers.com.
Book design by Sonia Chaghatzbanian
The text for this book is set in Celestia Antiqua Std.
Manufactured in the United States of America
First Edition
10 9 8 7 6 5 4 3 2 1
Library of Congress Cataloging-in-Publication Data
Names: Atkins, Jeannine, 1953- author.
Title: Stone mirrors : the sculpture and silence of Edmonia Lewis / Jeannine Atkins.
Description: First edition. | New York : Atheneum Books for Young Readers, [2017]
Summary: "A biographical novel in verse of a half Native American, half African American female sculptor, Edmonia Lewis, working in the years right after the Civil War"—Provided by publisher. | Includes bibliographical references and index.
Identifiers: LCCN 2016003598
ISBN 978-1-4814-5905-1
ISBN 978-1-4814-5907-5 (eBook)
Subjects: LCSH: Lewis, Edmonia—Juvenile fiction. | CYAC: Novels in verse. | Lewis, Edmonia—Fiction. | Women sculptors—Fiction. | Sculptors—Fiction. | BISAC: JUVENILE FICTION / Biographical / United States. | JUVENILE FICTION / Girls & Women. | JUVENILE FICTION / Stories in Verse.
Classification: LCC PZ7.5.A85 St 2016 | DDC [Fic]—dc23
LC record available at https://lccn.loc.gov/2016003598

For Margo Culley and Julia Demmin,
who showed me the importance of
hidden history

Oberlin, Ohio
1862-1863

Forbidden

Old branches crack as Edmonia breaks
a path through the woods. She wants
to outrun fury, or at least make a distance
between herself and the poison spoken
at Oberlin. The school is a shop where she can't buy,
a supper she's never meant to taste,
a holiday she can't celebrate
though she doesn't want to be left out.

She runs under trees taller than those in town,
where they're sawed into lumber,
turned into tables, rifles, or walls.
These woods are as close to home
as she may ever again get.
When she was given a chance to go
to boarding school, her aunts' farewell was final.
People who move into houses
with hard walls don't return to homes
that can be rolled and carried on backs.

Edmonia crouches to touch tracks
of birds and swift squirrels sculpted in snow,
the split hearts of deer hooves.
Boot prints are set far enough apart
to tell her the trespasser is tall,
shallow enough to guess he's slender.

Her cold breath stops, like ice.
She looks up at a deer whose dark gaze
binds them, turns into trust.
Then a branch breaks. The deer flees.

Hands

Brush rustles. A boy lopes through a clearing.
His hair shines like straw in sun. He says,
Hello. I've seen you at school.
Aren't you friends with Helen and Christine?

With Helen. Maybe. We live in the same dormitory.
Friend isn't from her first language.
She recognizes Seth as one of the boys,
about seventeen, in the class ahead of hers
and just behind those enrolled in the college.
She looks, as the deer taught her, for signs
of danger beyond weapons or words.

They say you make your own rules,
Seth says. *I see they're right.*
You're not supposed to be in the woods.

Or alone with a boy. *Neither are you.*
She was raised to respect fire, fast water,
and heights. But some school rules seem
like ropes meant to bind, choke, or trip
rather than keep someone safe. The woods
are her refuge from the school famous as the first
to open to both boys and girls,
white and colored,
rich and poor,

the good and the better-be-grateful,
though the lines between them are as firm as fences. ˇ

The trees call me, Seth says.

She looks up into the boughs. Is he teasing?
Or does he mean that trees call with
a hush and hum that never needs translation?
Each room at school—art, composition, geometry—
has its own language. Maybe the woods do, too.

I *read Hiawatha,* he says. *Was your life like that?*
Is it true you used to live outside?

When most people ask where she came from,
the question draws a line between them.
Most strangers want only a slip of a story,
like those the aunts who raised her gave tourists
to go with the deerskin moccasins
and sweetgrass baskets they bought,
reminders that history is as fragile as the present.

But Seth's voice is soft as an opening door.
He seems to ask about the past not to measure,
but to touch. There's no quiz in his eyes,
no examination of the pink-brown terrain of her palms,
the geography of her twisting hair.

She says, In winter, we stretched strips of bark
over trees young enough to bend, and slept
with our feet toward the fire in the middle.

I wish I could live like that. Seth raises
his voice. Or run away and help crush the Rebs,
never mind what my father says.

They walk silently a while to honor the dead
or missing slaves and soldiers.
They stop at the edge of the woods.
Smoke stains the sky. A train whistle blasts.
Small animals scurry across the field.

Seth crouches and holds his hand out flat,
as one would with salt for a horse,
as if he could tempt a hare back to the woods.
Here, homes are hidden—
burrows under snow, or in the hollows of trees—
as if secrets and dangers can't be the same.

Snowflakes start to fall. She and Seth walk again.
Their breath claims the same rhythm
before a waterfall frozen in mid-motion,
its power and old noise half-hidden.
A brook below trickles over rocks
and around small islands of ice.

Seth's eyes, green as the forest at dusk,
cast a spell. The wool of his jacket
mixes with the scent of his skin,
earthy and vaguely sweet, like clover.
He leans forward, offers a warm mouth.
Chickadees swoop and chirp.
Wind rattles dried grasses.

Edmonia hears another branch split.
Or is that the sound of old rules breaking?
Her breath unstitches.
She slips off a mitten.
Their fingers wind together.
Her small hand feels safe as an egg
within the nest of his wide one.
She feels a new pulse in her palm
keeping time with the snowflakes
melting on her face.

Their hands around each other's become
the warmest spot in the woods.

The First Promise

Before starting on separate paths back to the school,
Seth says, *Don't tell anyone.*

Edmonia's breath flows smoothly as a needle
through cloth. Her self fits within her skin
the way moccasins mold to feet,
a river wends through land,
or a crow slices her shape through the sky.

She says, I *won't tell.* Ever since
she heard how her mother invited a man heading north
—a man who was free, but a dangerous color—
into her bark house, Edmonia understood
that hiding and courage were part of love.

Old Stories

Edmonia can keep secrets. She doesn't speak
of her father, who, not long before her mother died,
left Edmonia with brown skin, round eyes, a wide mouth,
and not one memory. Still, his name is part of hers.
She won't speak of manitous, good spirits
who may stay within stone, but might warn
with a cracking branch. Her aunts taught her much
that they warned could be ruined by revelation.

Edmonia won't won't even whisper what her aunts held close.
But she wishes she could hint about the kiss
to the girls who share a room upstairs. Helen and Christine
like tales of forbidden romance: Romeo and Juliet
defying their families, Hiawatha and Minnehaha
marrying despite fighting between Ojibwe and Sioux,
Cleopatra luring a Roman into a barge
filled with gold and roses, forgetting
her country, careless that she was queen.

Portraits

The art room is undivided by chairs set in rows.
It smells of charcoal sticks and spiral shavings
from pencils sharpened with knives.
Landscapes are pinned to the walls.
White plaster busts of heads with empty eyes
and casts of hands and feet fill the shelves.
Nothing is shown of the body between.
Only after long practice on what's flat
are the older students allowed to work with clay.
They claim an art that takes up space
like the deerskin her aunts sculpted into shoes,
the baskets they wove from broken willow branches.

Edmonia and Helen work alone late in the afternoon.
Drawing is an invitation to someone
taking shape under a pencil
to come close enough to reveal what matters most.
But Edmonia's hand balks at the drawn shoulders.
She says, *Our teacher is a snake.*
He said the arms looked too soft,
and the hair couldn't possibly be Cleopatra's.

He criticizes everything, Helen says. *That's his job.*
Though he can be bitter. I think he imagined himself
as a real sculptor. No one wants to teach girls.

Are all these his work? Edmonia looks around
at plaster casts of Greek and Roman gods and goddesses.
Nobody could claim to know the shapes of their noses
or the texture of their hair. *I'll change Cleopatra to a goddess.*

These are copies he collected. All made by men in Europe.
Helen's short sentence holds a lot of history.
I want to see museums there one day.

I thought you wanted to show your work in one.

Yes, times are changing.
Wasn't Cleopatra eighteen when she became queen?
We have two years to become famous.
Helen puts down her pencil, the same blue as her eyes.
We shouldn't be late for supper. And I need
to get ready for the dance. You should come, too.
I mean to supper. You can't afford another demerit.

I'm almost done. Edmonia draws a circle in the hands
of her goddess, as if she's holding the world.
That's better than being able to attend a dance,
though she imagines her feet fast on the floor,
a boy's arm warming her waist.

After Helen leaves, she picks up some clay,
molds Seth's face, then presses the clay back
to possibility. Nobody should see what she touched.

She looks through the window, past the field
where she and Seth ducked through twilight,
holding a shiver of skin on skin in soft twined fists.

Saturday Afternoon

Edmonia gets to the table on time. But the next day,
the bell for study hour has tolled before she enters
the room she shares with Ruth. Two beds are checkered
with faded squares of fabric cut from old dresses
neither roommate recognizes. Edmonia picks up
a paper swan that had been slipped under the door.
She unfolds and flattens the note,
reads Helen's words across the wings:
A lovely dance last night. So silly you couldn't go.
Christine arranged for a sleigh today
with two handsome escorts. Come advise on fashion?

I'm going upstairs, Edmonia says. *Helen needs help*
choosing what to wear for a sleigh ride.

We're supposed to be studying.
You're not a servant. Ruth scowls.
Those girls are too flighty to manage horses.

I expect the boys will take the reins.

Boys and no chaperone? Ruth shakes her head.

You have a fellow, Edmonia points out.

And you take advantage that Father Keep
is hard of hearing. No one else would let people like us
study right along with white students.
And you spend too much time with those girls.
If there's trouble, you'll be first to get blamed.

Lectures like that makes it hard for them to like you.

The good people of Boston didn't raise
scholarship money so I could have friends, Ruth says.
We vowed when we came here to be of a character
that no one can criticize. And don't tell me
you're an exception. No matter how many stories
you tell about your past life in the forest,
they don't see halves.
You and I are the same in their eyes.

I'm not like you. Edmonia's older brother
sent money he made mining gold
so she could enroll, though she hasn't heard
from him since. My mother was Indian.
And my father a freedman.

Who happened to be walking north?
Of course he told people there were no papers

claiming he belonged to someone else.
It's what any colored man would say to stay alive.

Edmonia flings open the door.
The world is changing.

The String of Pearls

Helen's petticoat swirls over her ankles as she spins
to shut the door. She waves two dresses,
whose hems skim the floor. *What do you think?*
My poplin with puffed sleeves or the blue taffeta?

I *like them both.* Edmonia smooths the dress
she wears six days a week. The room
smells of cinnamon, nutmeg, and cider mulling
on the bright stove. Helen and Christine
come from families who don't skimp on coal.

A *hoop skirt flatters the waist.* Christine takes a curling iron
off the cast iron stove. She winds a strand of her blond hair
around the rod. *But when it comes between crinoline*
and a boy being able to reach around my waist,
I *cast my vote for dress reform. Besides, no one will see.*
We'll be under furs or quilts. With luck, the boys will be, too.
Christine turns to Edmonia. I *heard you have an admirer.*

Edmonia's face turns warm. Had Seth told
someone what he'd asked her not to tell?

A boy named Thomas? Christine adds. *Who sends*
around petitions to start a colored army?

They were talking about Ruth.

Edmonia doesn't point out they're not alike.
She picks up a silver-handled hairbrush
and walks around Helen, examining
the shape of each side of her head.
She braids, twists, and tugs the brown hair
still straighter, pierces it with pins to clip it in place.

Helen holds up a looking glass and frowns.
It *needs something.*

*You need something. Edmonia, will you pour
us some cider?* Christine says.

Cleopatra wove pearls through her hair.
Edmonia stirs and pours the hot cider.

I *have that necklace from my father!* Helen sifts
through keepsakes on her bureau: a music box,
scissors shaped like a bird, and lily of the valley scent.
She finds a cedarwood box and opens the lid.
Its emptiness fills the room.

Helen's gaze rises to Edmonia, whose teeth ache.
On the top of the bureau are pledges
of lasting devotion: locks of hair twined
into charms, cards with pressed wildflowers.
A cameo pin has a profile carved
in pale stone; only half the face shows.

China Teacups and the Queen of Egypt

Helen's eyes blur back to blue.
She bends to open a drawer. *Christine, I knew*
when you told me to hide my jewelry
I'd forget where I put it. Helen reaches
under rolled stockings and gloves
to pull out a necklace. She laughs,
as if no one had heard accusation
flicker over her tongue. *I wasn't hiding*
it from thieves. But such trinkets are forbidden
in school so they don't cause trouble.

My father gave me a necklace, too. Edmonia stands
straight as a guest alert to hints she's stayed too long.
It was made of garnets. You can find them
near the river. I'll put those pearls in your hair.
She twists them through smooth strands. Helen flinches
and sips from a china cup painted with roses,
then purses her lips. *The cider is sour.*
Did you put something in this?

Spices, Christine says. *And a bit of something*
my Albert says will make you fuss less about what's proper.

Like Cleopatra's love potions? Helen swallows.

She had to lure suitors? Christine asks. *I thought*

she was beautiful, clever, and rich.

She wanted men on the wrong side. Romans
kneeling at her feet, feeding her peeled grapes.

I expect that wasn't all they were doing.
Christine pours more cider in their cups.
Didn't she murder her brother and sister?

They say "assassinate" in history class, Helen says.
But yes. And she put poison in a rival city's water.

Nobody rules by being kind, Christine says.
Didn't she kill herself? Like Romeo and Juliet?

She didn't poison herself because of love gone wrong,
Helen says. Rome was invading her country.
Her maids snuck in an asp curled among figs in a basket.

Why would she kill herself?

If the Romans won, they'd mock and chain her.
Maybe put her in prison.
Helen picks up the mirror again.
You can't really see the pearls.
They must have looked better on Cleopatra,
white pearls and black hair together.

She had black hair? Christine asks.
Of course, she was queen of Egypt. I forgot
that's in Africa. But who cares where she lived?
You two can laugh, but my Albert doesn't mind
that I'm no genius in geography. He and I
will get cozy in the back of the sleigh. Helen, you can
recite all your daffodils and nightingales and shores
of Gitche Gumee, while Seth minds the horses.

You're riding with Seth?
Edmonia blurts out, *He likes me!*

Don't be foolish, Helen says.

Christine makes a sound like a laugh. *That's all*
my father needs to hear: a romance
between a white boy and a colored girl.

Edmonia hears a cup settle on the table.
Have more. Don't. Stop. Listen.
Outside, sleigh runners scrape packed snow.

The Window

Edmonia leans on the glass pane,
watches the green-eyed boy
in a brown jacket check a horse's harness.
Helen takes a seat in front, pulls up a quilt.
She stares straight ahead as if already watching
for half-hidden dips in the road.

Seth looks up at the window.
Do his eyes widen at the sight of Edmonia?
Is he trying to tell her this ride is a duty,
a favor to a friend? She trusts
eyes and hands more than mouths.

Seth snaps the reins. The horses bolt
past trees forced to grow straight as fences.
Snow flares and flashes from under the runners
like a swan's spreading wings.

Mythology

Edmonia doesn't see Seth, Helen, or Christine in chapel
the next morning. The girls aren't at Sunday dinner.
After the other boarders wash dishes, they sew
blue shirts for soldiers and write letters home.
Edmonia's aunts roll up their homes each season
and follow signs from rivers and stars.
Edmonia writes, then burns her letters.
Smoke is as useful as stamps she can't afford.

Her past once seemed steady. Now it flickers, as uncertain
as the future. School is a tightrope. Each step is a chance
to fall. Her arms and legs turn straw-stuffed
when kept too long where walls and furniture stay still.
She needs to get out. Would Seth be in the woods?
Would he tell the truth under the trees?

She starts past the road, but the wind is bitter and her shawl
is thin. She hurries back to shelter in the art room.
On the walls, myths turn as tangible as tables.
Drawings show girls becoming birds, stars, sunflowers,
or stone. Daphne transforms into a tree.
A vain weaver grows spider legs.
Names and even a person can change in an instant.

Edmonia can't afford to waste paper, but rips up
her drawing. Cleopatra shows through, or does the face

of her goddess look too much like Helen's?
She borrows Helen's cakes of colors, starts painting a bird,
but art needs a story. She squints one eye, tilts the brush
to pry out the moment when a god turned into a swan.

Did his belly ache, his throat pinch, as arms widened
to wings? Did Zeus mourn the loss of hands and language,
hail an elegant neck? She dabs a brush on cerulean blue
for shadows as skin turns to feathers. As she paints the beak
she hears the part of the story she missed:
This was a disguise so he could attack a girl desperate
to escape. He wasn't a swan but a monster.
When did she learn to take the side of a brute?

Chapel bells ring for afternoon prayers.
Edmonia's absence will earn her another demerit,
but she must finish what she started.
She's painting shimmer on the dull orange beak
when the door opens. A gust of wind
stirs pencil shavings. It's Seth, bringing back
the warm shiver of his palm on hers.
Warmth spreads through her face, then turns chill
as he says, *Helen and Christine are sick.*
Albert and I left them for the night at Christine's house.

What's wrong? She pushes down the hair
above her forehead, which twists like flames.

They got sick in the sleigh,
which I couldn't stop in time for them to get out.
Christine's father helped them inside.
Something was wrong even before.
People say anything in such a state.
I said it wasn't your fault.

What wasn't my fault?

Bells ring for supper, so she hardly hears
Seth ask, What did you give them to drink?

Nothing. They said your friend gave them a potion.
Is it the crackling of sticks turning to ash
in the stove that make her belly clench,
or the way his eyes turn to the dim green of a swamp?
Maybe it's just dusk creeping through the frosted windows.

She opens the door, slams it behind Seth.
An icicle falls from the eaves,
cracking on frozen ground.

Grace

The sun's last light turns fields of snow pink.
Shadows darken. She dashes into the dormitory.
Three straight-backed chairs at the table are empty.
Nine pairs of hands folded for prayer thud softly.
The girls' eyes shift to gray-haired Father Keep
as Edmonia takes one chair, waiting
for him to scold her for being tardy.

Instead, he shuts his eyes, slips off
his wire-rimmed spectacles. His wife bows her head,
too, as he prays for President Lincoln,
the Union troops, and the girls' absent families.
He thanks the Lord for the bread they're about to eat
and says, *Bless those not here tonight.*

Amen, the girls murmur. Then Clara asks,
Are Helen and Christine dead?

Mercy, where did you hear such a thing?
Father Keep signals his wife to serve sausages,
stewed cabbage, parsnips, and toasted bread.
*They're ill, but are getting the best of care at the home
of Miss Ennes, which is all that need be said.
Take care that no rumors spread from here.
Not in your talk, nor in your letters home.*
Father Keep twines his wrinkled fingers into an orb

he sets on the edge of the table, and bows his head.
Does fear narrow the lines between his tensed fingers?

Edmonia bites a corner of toast, which catches in her throat.

Paper Swans

After wiping the dishes, Edmonia slips upstairs
to Helen's and Christine's room. Where did
they put those herbs? Should she hide them
so no one gets caught? She looks on the bureau
where the pearls form a circle, like a song.
She pries open a tin that smells of stale fudge,
and flips through Helen's Bible with a flock
of family names written at the front.

She looks through a book of poems, stopping
on the page where Hiawatha mourns Minnehaha.
Edmonia hadn't paid enough attention
to this particular poem, or the ends
of Juliet's and Cleopatra's stories:
the betrayals, lost words, poison.

She finds a piece of paper. She writes
—*Get well*—and creases the paper
into a small sculpture of a swan.

The Visitor

Returning to the dormitory from morning chapel,
Edmonia and the other girls see a horse,
breathing heavily, tied to a porch rail.

Clara says, *Helen and Christine must be back.*
I knew they'd be all right.

Ruth points out, *They wouldn't come on one horse.*

Harriet Wright fetches unfrozen water for the animal.
The others rush into the parlor.
A man with hair slightly paler than Christine's yells,
What kind of school lets girls and boys ride off
with nobody watching?

We're gravely concerned, Mr. Ennes, Father Keep says.

Are Helen and Christine better? Edmonia asks.

They're still alive this morning, bless the Lord.
My wife prays our daughter sees another day.
Mr. Ennes's eyes darken as they leave Edmonia's.
I knew you let in coloreds, but no one told me
they'd live with everyone else.
Do they eat from the same table?
Don't tell me they sleep in the same rooms.

Edmonia was in their bedroom. Mary Ellen speaks up.
I heard screams before they left.

Then it's true! Mr. Ennes's pale face turns crimson.
My wife told me to stay calm and watch my tongue.
She didn't want to believe anyone would hurt her daughter.
But our Christine claims that colored girl
who calls herself an Injun poisoned her.

This is a serious accusation, sir! Father Keep says.

There's guilt all over her face,
Mr. Ennes says. *I have my proof.*

She was in their room last night, too.
Mary Ellen's voice is shrill.

I *wasn't!* Edmonia bolts past her bedroom,
then up the stairs to Helen's and Christine's room.
Surely neither could have blamed her.
There must be a mistake—but what if there wasn't?
She can't remember what she's looking for,
but knocks things off the bureau.
Sewing scissors, jewelry, paper swans,
and the silver-handled hairbrush scatter.
A china teacup breaks.

Girls gather in the doorway.
Mary Ellen shrieks, *What are you doing?*
I'm getting Father Keep.

Edmonia raises her fist.

Ruth grabs her elbow, says, *She's returning a book*
before someone accuses her of stealing it.

Be quiet, Mary Ellen, Harriet demands.
They're probably not even sick.
Helen takes to bed every month when she's indisposed.
And Christine turns everything into theater.

Edmonia bends over, picks up the pearls, cameo pin,
and crane-shaped scissors from the pine plank floor.
She sweeps up shards of china, shining like eyes.
She presses paper swans through the stove's grate,
where they burn into black and beak-colored embers.

Wilderness

That night moonlight shines through the window.
The bureau Edmonia shares with Ruth is bare on top.
The only charms she has are hidden, a pair
of small moccasins her mother stitched before she died.

Edmonia puts on a nightgown, pulls her wool blanket
into a small tent that won't keep out fury, fear,
or the memory of clattering china teacups.
She tells Ruth, *Seth said that Helen and Christine*
were in no state to know or tell the truth.

What were you doing talking to Seth? Never mind.
Don't let anyone know you were alone with a boy.

Don't tell me you're never alone with Thomas.

We do nothing we shouldn't. Ruth pulls pins
from her hair, so it swells behind her shoulders.
She awkwardly unfastens the long line
of buttons down the back of her dress,
which smells of starch. She won't ask for help.
I know you think I'm churchy and prim,
but I'm not blind. Oberlin may be a temperance town,
but neighbors sell jugs to anyone who asks.
I've seen folks fall flat on their face, but get up

the next day with no recollection
of all the fool things they said or did.

They didn't know the tea would make them ill.
No one knew. I didn't mean . . .
Edmonia fumbles for words.
Even memory is not on her side,
but a trap and a door, lock and key.

I heard you were talking about potions
and poison, Ruth says.

We were talking about Cleopatra!

A murderer.

That's history.

Nothing is over. They'll think the worst.
Don't tell anyone you were there.

I didn't do anything wrong.
Her back teeth ache. Did she want
Helen to get sick or embarrass herself?
That wasn't guilt, but it wasn't innocence either.

If Christine or Helen lied, they'll regret it
and tell the truth. They're my friends.

Friends! A white girl always puts herself first.
Hagar probably thought Abraham's wife, Sarah,
was her friend until she was banished to the wilderness.

Who's Hagar?

You should spend less time drawing and more
with your Bible. Ruth looks at the book heavy
with stories about the good waiting
for their rewards, and poetry about angels
hidden in beggars and strangers.

I hear enough of men giving advice
in chapel, Edmonia says.

The Bible shows girls like us. Ruth touches her hair,
which springs into a dark cloud around her face.
Sarah couldn't conceive, but Abraham wanted a son.
He went into the tent of her slave, Hagar.
She grew great with child. Sarah got jealous.
Hagar was sent into the wilderness,
and told never to return.

Rumor

The blue sky looks scrubbed. It stretches over rows
of trees and white houses, similar as stamps,
in the flat town that was planned for perfection.
Walking on shoveled walkways,
Edmonia notes who steps aside, who leans away.
Some boys wear linen jackets and girls silk dresses
to avoid cotton picked by slaves. Every day
students pray to be good. Silence casts a spell of equality:
No one should point to differences in color or
between students on scholarships and those who pay.

Don't say anything to anyone. Act as if
nothing's changed. Ruth walks close, but glances away.

Edmonia guesses she's looking for her beau,
though Thomas is in the college program with classes
on another schedule. *I should have stayed in our room.*

None of us can afford to miss a class, Ruth says.
Ever since I heard that Senator Calhoun challenged
Northerners to show him a colored person
who could conjugate Greek verbs,
I swore I'd learn Greek and Latin
and one day teach those languages, too.

I'm not like you. Edmonia stops talking
as Seth, his light hair shining, strides toward her.
He says, *I heard Helen and Christine are better.*
But they won't come back to school.
They're taking their accusation to court.

This can't come to trial just on the word of two foolish girls,
Ruth exclaims. *Who I expect were drinking.*

Albert brought a jug of apple wine, Seth says.
And maybe some sort of herb he got from the college boys.

You need to tell Christine's father, Ruth says.

He'd cane her, Seth replies.

Edmonia spins around as a boy calls, *Watch out*
for the wild Indian. Don't take a drink from her.

Ruth tugs Edmonia's arm
to move her farther down the walkway.
The boy steps closer, calls toward their backs,
They're plotting who to poison next.

Rage rolls down Edmonia's chest and into her hands.
Don't you dare say anything about Ruth.

You gave them an Indian potion. Murderer!

Edmonia flings a fist at the boy's pale chin,
hurls herself upon him, pounding
his chest as he tries to shove her off.

Stop it! Harriet, Seth, Clara, and others circle them.
Edmonia punches and pants with unfinished fury
as she's pulled to her feet.
Chapel bells clang for the start of classes.

She's crazy! a boy shouts.

As everyone else hurries toward schoolrooms,
Ruth brushes snow and grit off Edmonia's shawl.
Never mind what people say.

Edmonia pulls her shawl close. She can't forget
every right or wrong name.

The Defense

Edmonia moves her pencil to mirror the silhouettes
of animals and trees, but a flat world under her hands
offers no haven. She looks out the one window
in their room, then rests her head on the desk.
The wood is dark from letters she burned,
nicked from pen knives. She pushes aside
Ruth's books, an inkwell, and a few stones
that sparkle with mica and marks
that look like small footprints.

Memory skates around thoughts:
It's *not my fault.*
Of course it's my fault.
She can't keep her balance.
She shouldn't have told Ruth she spoke with Seth.
Is she being punished for breaking
her promise not to tell?
Or should she have said more?
Memory won't mind borders.
Who said: *Drink?* Who said: *Stop?*
She wants to sleep, cross the lines between
truth and forgetting, daytime and dreaming.

She hears a knock. Harriet opens the door.
Father Keep is with Mr. Langston,
the colored lawyer who knows President Lincoln!
Edmonia, they want to see you!

Edmonia hurries to the library, curtsies to the man
she heard speak on the courthouse steps the day
John Brown was hanged. She's forgotten
Mr. Langston's words about the freedom fighter,
but not the way hundreds of white folks looked up
and listened to the tall, well-dressed lawyer.

Your client, Miss Lewis, Father Keep introduces her.

I consider myself to be representing this academy and college,
Mr. Langston replies. *If it were not for Oberlin,
I could never have become a lawyer. If this young lady
is convicted of attempted murder, who would send
their children here? But I intend to win this case
and keep everything out of the newspapers, too.
We're fortunate to have an editor in town who's sympathetic,
but I hate to think what they'd do with this in Cleveland.*

Cleveland. Oh, dear. Father Keep nudges up his spectacles.

I didn't do anything! Edmonia cries.

That's just the kind of outburst I can't have in court.
Mr. Langston raises a well-groomed hand, proof
he doesn't pick cotton the way his mother did,
evidence that times can change. *If all goes as I plan,
you won't testify. Silence is the best defense.*

I *have to tell everyone what happened.*
Can she? She's spoken English for years,
but she's not fluent with words that fall
between Yes and No.
She has a grasp of words
for action and what can be held,
but not *Maybe* or *Sometimes,* words
used to smudge or straddle fact and falsehoods.
I *have to talk to Helen and Christine.*
Make them remember I was their friend.

We're not dealing with rational people, Miss Lewis.
Yesterday, Mr. Ennes chased me with his rifle.
Fortunately, he has terrible aim.

Christine's *father tried to shoot you?*
Father Keep stands up. John, *my dear Lord!*
What did the sheriff do?

I *didn't report it. Union soldiers in the South*
withstand more than one misfired bullet.

But *this isn't a war,* Father Keep says.

I *can understand how it might feel to be afraid that*
your daughter is dying. Some good people in this town
have sent sons to war. They may never come back.
Townsfolk think they've made enough sacrifices

for our people, and are angry that some seem ungrateful.
But I'm going to win this case. Mr. Langston's back
is perfectly straight as he turns to Edmonia.
They want you in jail until you appear in court,
though there aren't cells for young ladies.
I promised them you won't leave here until the trial,
except for church on Sunday mornings.

Rumor already binds her breath.
She won't ask what will happen if he fails.

What's Possible

After Edmonia reports what was said,
Ruth paces across their small room,
says, *You can't even attend classes? That's awful,
though Mr. Langston must know what he's doing.*
Thomas says he works with Mr. Frederick Douglass,
*campaigning for colored men to be allowed to enlist
in the army. Thomas would be the first to sign on.*

Wouldn't you worry? Edmonia welcomes
a chance to talk about anyone but herself.

*I'd be proud. Though it's not as if we have what they call
an understanding, not yet. We're at this school
from the goodness of people who wanted to give us a chance
to make the world better, not have a merry time.*
Thomas means to prove his older brother's death
*was not in vain. He was shot while helping
John Brown try to take weapons for a rebellion.*

Edmonia runs her fingertips from an ear to a shoulder.
Did John Brown imagine a rope around his neck?
Or did he think death was impossible, too?
She closes her eyes to envision his face,
wishes she could draw his portrait, unafraid.

Here, every precious pencil and sheet of paper
must be accounted for, but no one can take away

her hands. She curves her palms and bends her thumbs
to sculpt air into doors she'll stride through.
Even as she shapes beauty no one else can yet see,
her hands are cold with dread.

Ice and Glass

Chapel bells mark the start of classes
Edmonia doesn't attend.
Her belly is heavy as stone,
her chest strung like a slingshot.
Her throat feels as if it were gnawed by
dangerous spirits who tear skin and flesh,
who took her mother, even most of her memory.
There's no end to their greed.

Every day the room seems smaller.
Edmonia tries to blow a clear space on the iced-over window.
Once if she stood still and stared,
beauty startled into view. That's gone.
Her breath taps inside her chest like snowmelt
to the rhythm of *run, run.*
Should she leave town?
Any path would be narrow
as flames from a birchbark torch.
She lies down and dreams of her aunts, who praised
her older brother for seeking a new life out west.
They told her no one can go back.
Once traders brought in beads,
women stopped decorating moccasins with quills,
making pictures of turtles, loons, otters,
and starflowers they'd seen in dreams.

After women could buy cloth, thread, and needles,
they rarely sewed deerskin. Steel needles are sharper than bone.

Even as she grew up, the past was breaking.
Her aunts sold its pieces spread on blankets,
turning what was scavenged into mementos and toys.
They sewed pin cushions and small pillows,
stitched English words they couldn't read:
Niagara Falls and *Remember Me*.

Edmonia takes out the moccasins her mother made
when she was a baby. The beaded blue flowers
and fish-shaped leaves are beautiful, but there's a hole
by the heel. Ojibwe mothers left an imperfection
to trick spirits into thinking an infant was unloved,
not worth snatching for the long journey to the other side.

Edmonia puts back the moccasins. She misses the taste
of fish cooked over flames with mountain mint,
fried pumpkin blossoms, wild rice, and dark berries.
She kneels for the particular silence called prayer.
Instead of words from people who built ceilings
between themselves and sky,
laid floors to block the land's voice,
an old Ojibwe plea runs like a pulse through her.

The words disappear under memories of girls' voices.
Drink more. That's enough. Stop.
Who said what? Voices cross into each other
like nightmares that scream through days, too.

Her breath slams against the walls.
Edmonia breaks her comb. The snap calms her,
but she needs more. She opens scissors,
studies the tarnished blades, then drops them.
She runs her fingers down the window locked by ice.
Does she hear wind from the woods
or is someone calling her name?
The voice sounds like Seth's.
She looks through the glass into darkness,
past the field where dried cornstalks pierce snow.

When the World Changed

Edmonia twists on her shawl, fastens her gloves,
unlatches the door, steps outside.
An owl calls to another.
She walks toward the field
under a crescent moon and scattered stars.
The sky swoops like another shawl around her shoulders.

A branch snaps.
She steps back. Too late.

As if darkness isn't disguise enough,
men have tied cloth over their faces.
One grabs her arms,
claps a hand over her mouth.
Other men wrestle rough cloth over her head.
We'll show her what's wrong and right.

White men's voices sound too much the same.
Are there five or six who pull her
across old corn stalks and hard snow? Eight?
She smells whiskey, sweat, damp wool.
The sharp point of a boot jabs her ankle.

No! she cries, then *Naw! Booni'!*
She grabs snow and a stone.
She drops it. Too many hands grip her arms.

Fists drum: *You don't belong here.*
Shoving her to the ground, one man turns
into a flock, tearing clothing that's around her legs,
arms, and vulnerable neck.
Her voice turns to a rasp
as she begs in two languages for mercy.

Cold wings sweep. Beaks snap.
Wild swans or men
gnaw her throat
shred her voice
feast on her heart
hungrier with each bite.

A boot slams on her thigh.
Someone pulls down her stockings,
jams ice between her legs.
Blood melts the snow.
She reaches up.
Her own shouts
prayers
promises
lies
begging
curses
shatter on sky.

Distant stars mock with their blinking.
The black sky refuses to answer.

Again, she reaches for a rock.
Her hand curls around nothing.

The New Story

Where did the light come from?
Edmonia tries to push away palms,
but her arms are bound. She cries, *Go away!*

Edmonia, you're safe. You're in your own bed.

It's the soft voice of a girl, but Edmonia
feels a man's weight claim her name,
smells his sharp, foul breath.
She knows this room, but the pinch
of a cage around her chest is foreign.
Pain shoots through her right leg
as she tries to sit,
then collapses like a stone girl.

Rescuers found you in a field,
Ruth says. *Don't you remember?*
I told Father Keep you weren't in our room.
I knew you wouldn't run away, not without a good-bye
to me or taking your old moccasins.
They rang church bells to call men to look for you.

Edmonia shifts her hand to a damp cloth between her legs.
Her hope that the night was nightmare collapses.
She tries to remember what happened,

then stops. Her eyes sting.
She fumbles with the cloth bands around her arms.

I wrapped you to break your fever. I'll take them off now.
I've got the woodstove burning as high as it will go.
My sister had a fever like this in the middle
of a Virginia summer. She couldn't stop shaking.
Edmonia, did you see who did it?

It was dark. They threw burlap over my head.

They? Ruth's voice splits.

I heard six different voices.

Monsters!

I wasn't supposed to go outside.

It's a crime to hurt, not a crime to be hurt.
Those men must be punished, Ruth says.

They won't be. Even though Edmonia might
be able to identify them from the shapes of their hands
and their voices. *No one can know what happened.*

Like an artist drawing a line meant to direct eyes
another way, she struggles onto her elbows,
reaches down to grab and turn her ankle.

What are you doing?

They only see the surface, Edmonia says.
If something's broken, no one will look beyond.

*In the dark and cold, I don't think the rescuers could tell
the difference between melting snow
and freezing blood. They only know you were beaten.*

I won't look weak.

*This isn't your fault. But you're right. It's better
if no one knows. Too many blame everything on the girl,
even back in Bible days. No girl with a choice
would lift her skirt for an old man
who wouldn't look her in the eye.*

I'm not like Hagar. Edmonia grabs her foot,
which Ruth takes between her strong hands.

There's no shame in a sprained ankle,
Ruth says, then twists Edmonia's ankle hard.

Both girls bite their lips, but gasp as they hear a crack.
Edmonia's jaw aches as she holds back screams.

We'll tell everyone you can't walk,
Ruth says. *That's why you'll stay
in this room until you're ready to leave.
If I thought there was any justice it would be different.*

Edmonia stares at her dress, drying on a chair
by the hearth. Ruth must have scrubbed
it with a fury while she slept. She left the sleeves
neatly crossed as if nothing had ever happened.

Edmonia says, *Give me my moccasins.*

Ruth opens the middle drawer, hands her
slippers so small they both fit on one palm.

Edmonia holds them to her face, breathes
deerskin-scented air. *Burn them.*

Aren't they all you have from your mother?

Holes or missing stitches didn't help.
She insists, *Burn them. Please.*

Old Gifts

Leaning on proof she already was punished,
not knowing if that will matter,
Edmonia shifts her crutches, making her way
past colored people in the back rows. Father Keep
and teachers crowd benches in the front. Behind
them sit students—is that Seth?—and men who work
in the sawmill, apothecary, general store, or on farms.

Helen and Christine keep their eyes fixed ahead
as if they don't recognize her.
Helen's cheeks are sunken, the rims of her eyes pink.
Trust was never part of what they called friendship,
which was a tent constructed of promises, jokes, dares,
and rare confessions. These girls will stay sixteen,
sitting still beside white fathers who once built
them doll houses and swings, who traded strings of pearls
for promises to be good, who believe them
or pretend to. The girls lean against mothers
who buttoned the backs of their collars and twisted
their fine hair, pinned every strand into place.

The Trial

The lawyer feints, his hands blurring like those of a magician
with a wand, conjuring a spell from what can't be seen.
Mr. Langston repeats: *No evidence.*
He won't say *murder*, or even *attempted*,
words that shape the silent breath
of everyone filling the biggest room in town.

Does the magic-maker believe his own words?
He chants names of poisons like charms,
and what each can or can't do,
a long story meant to illuminate
or set in shadows what was or wasn't in teacups.

Edmonia's name scrapes as if caught by brambles,
snagging her skirt, scratching her skin.
She can almost hear people thinking:
It was a mistake to let a girl like her
into a school like this.
In this town laid out precisely as a table,
with forks to the left, knives to the right,
people believe in two sides, guilt or innocence,
unlike the world,
where blood, snow, and earth become one.

Telling

That night in their room, Ruth asks,
When will you take the stand?

I might not. The lawyer doesn't want me to speak.
He hopes to win the case on lack of evidence.

That doesn't prove anything.

It can keep me out of jail.

You can tell me. What happened
that afternoon with Helen and Christine?

I poured what they asked for . . . Edmonia stops,
hears the spill of cider
or a click of a lock. *I shouldn't have . . .*
Memory isn't solid as stone,
but a river, wrecking its banks,
so she can't tell truth from lies.
Time and voices blur, while again
and again, men clutch and twist her hair,
which becomes a weapon, turned against her.
She can't tell their fingers from icicles.

It's all right. You're not alone.
Ruth leans toward her.
Let me tell you something.

No. Edmonia can hardly carry the weight
of her own memory. She can't bear another's.

Ruth catches her breath,
as if she just stopped running.

Everything She Knows and Doesn't Know

Edmonia pins her hair behind her head, still feeling
how it was pulled by strangers in the field,
used as a harness to hold her down.
She walks to the court for a second morning.

Her neck aches from looking up at the judge.
She squeezes the red mittens Mrs. Keep knit for her,
saying, *What a shame they never found your gloves.*

Edmonia wishes she were in the woods
or at least back where she handed sightseers
birchbark tipis and canoes small enough to sail on a palm.
Buyers, turning their backs to the waterfall's beauty
and danger, seemed to crave a glimpse
of her brown hand as much as a toy,
small enough to pocket and forget.
Cross-legged on a woven blanket, she took coins,
traced the embossed reliefs of a bird, star,
wreath, goddess. Even the metal pressed into profiles
can be turned over. What's unseen isn't gone.

Edmonia learned English from watching as well as listening,
puzzling out secrets behind crunching eyes or curling fists,
a talent useful here in court. She studies the ways
eyebrows slant, lines on foreheads clench,
how people peer without moving their necks or eyes,

secretly craving scandal and wreckage
more than justice, which is the same story every time.

Her face stays as still as her aunts kept theirs
when strangers picked up beaded belts or willow baskets,
then put them back down.
Stillness was a skill as much as the crafts.

The Second Evening

Edmonia moves Ruth's Bible, algebra book,
and Latin grammar from their desk. She leans
across it, watching the setting sun tangle in treetops,
darkness conceal the edge of the woods.
She sees Thomas bite an apple he hands to Ruth,
who tucks her chin to taste. She gives back the fruit,
her hands still curved as if to remember its shape.

Soon Ruth comes inside, drops her shawl,
opens a book, closes it, studies Edmonia.
There must be someone who can help.
Are your aunts still at Niagara Falls?
Do you know where your brother is?

Samuel said he'd write when he had money to send me.
Edmonia mailed a few letters, which were returned.
She supposes her brother moves from one riverbed or cliff
to another, but trusts he has her address and knows
she'd like word from him even if he can't send money.

Could she run away and search for her father?
Wouldn't he help? She doesn't even know
what he looks like. After fleeing north through the woods,
he must have glanced over his shoulder when he heard
sudden noises. Probably every colored man in Canada
was afraid of being followed. She couldn't approach
each one and ask, *Did you leave behind a daughter?*

Edmonia swallows hard. A beak seems to snap her throat,
a beast gnaws her belly. *I can't walk back in there.*
Even people who don't think I'm guilty want me to be.

You must be strong. Others have survived worse.

Don't tell me about Hagar.

I wasn't thinking about her.
Edmonia, if the worst happens,
you won't be like Cleopatra, will you?

You mean choose poison instead of prison?
Edmonia's face hardens. *She did the noble thing.*

She was wrong! And maybe we were, too,
not telling anyone about the brutes who attacked
you in the field. I hate that they're still free.

Nothing happened. Edmonia must hold the line
between the past and present. It may be all she has.

I thought it was strange that no one at the school called
the sheriff, or reported the men. Maybe it was courtesy.
They wanted to help put it behind you. But if your lawyer
is concerned that no one will send their children
to a school where someone attempts murder,

I suppose they also worry that no one might
go to a school where a girl was attacked in a field.

I'm all right.

Edmonia, you can confide in someone.
What starts out seeming like weakness
can turn to strength.

Telling is like laying out cloth so anyone can see
thin or rough spots where she might have made
a different choice. Blame is always close.
Edmonia says, *You know nothing about it.*

Ruth opens her mouth, turns her eloquent back.
Her straight spine is parallel to a row of buttons
that she manages alone every time.

Verdict

The hall is crowded. Is the world shrinking?
The tight, still necks show judgments as sharp
as those of the man in the robe, his pale hand by a gavel.
The lawyer stands straight as a post, raises a thick book.
The doctor never examined the contents of the patients' bowels
or stomachs. This medical text confirms that's the only way
to prove poisoning. Can the state of Ohio in good faith
convict someone of attempted murder with no proof?

Each word is a spider, catching Edmonia's breath
in its web. Edmonia looks at her lap. Once she was a child,
winding loops of string between two pairs of hands,
tugged in four directions. She spun swans opening wings,
rivers colliding, and people turning to animals.
Was that a stone or a door, land or sky?
Guessing was part of the game.
Candles, diamonds, cat's eyes, fish, stars, ladders,
and fences swallowed one another,
until the pictures shredded like clouds in the wind.

At last the judge meets the lawyer's gaze.
He dismisses the case for insufficient evidence.

Edmonia ducks under cheers, cries, gasps, shouts
of No! as if at the end of a game or fumbled magic act

that continues to distort what's seen or unseen,
a girl stumbling into a hole.

Father Keep shakes Mr. Langston's hand, turns
to Edmonia, warns, *You must stay*
on your best behavior. Nothing can go amiss.

People shove forward to shake her hand,
pat her head or shoulders. Every touch feels dangerous.
Beyond the shouts, silence stings like spoken judgments.
Edmonia reaches for her crutches, which clatter as they fall.

Boys bend to pick them up. Girls squeeze her arms.
I'm all right, she says, her words swept off
by the river of hands around her,
the cheers as if there were no difference between
lack of proof and innocence, which she still means to claim.
This isn't a victory, or even the end of a story.
Her chance to speak is gone.

The Pearls

Late that afternoon in her room,
Edmonia hears footsteps from the floor overhead.
Voices cross like a mother's and daughter's.
Drawers open and close. Helen must be packing
a hair-curling rod, silk dresses, rose-painted cups.

Edmonia hears only one pair of feet on the stairs.
She's surprised by the knock on her door,
stunned that she walks over and lifts the latch.

Helen doesn't step in, but stands wearing
a shawl and hat, her hands in her woolen muff,
all ready to go. Edmonia almost shuts the door,
but Helen steps forward. She whispers,
I'm glad you said nothing. You won't ever,
will you? My father would kill me
if he knew everything that happened.

She draws a hand from the muff and holds
out the string of pearls to Edmonia.
The gems are white on the surface,
crossed by the shadows and shine of water.
Someone could see or lose herself in that shimmer.

Edmonia keeps her hands still.

They're a gift, Helen explains,
as if Edmonia didn't speak this language.

She says, *I know what they are.*

Raising Her Voice

Some snow melts. The first crow returns.
It is the time when her aunts rolled up birchbark walls
to drag to a spot where they could tap maple trees
for sap to boil into sugar, turning the forest fragrant.

Every day is a new trial.
Edmonia's neck turns stiff from the stares
of students who sit behind her.
Words split in her ears, blur before her eyes.
She no longer needs crutches
as oak leaves grow to the size of squirrel paws,
the season to find a spot near a river
to fish with nets and spears
and plant squash and corn and beans.
By summer, Edmonia walks without a limp.

During the time of Leaves Turning, new girls move
into the room upstairs. One night,
Ruth says, *I heard Helen and Seth are engaged.*
I suppose that's to be expected, being discovered in a sleigh
without a chaperone. He's working for Helen's father.

Edmonia winces. *He wanted to join the Union Army.*

But he didn't. Ruth pats her hair like someone trying
to stop a fire. *And it's a shame we need even boys like him.*

He didn't really do anything wrong.

He did nothing right. You've been so quiet
these past months, Edmonia. It's not like you.

And it's not like you to raise your voice.
I didn't know you were angry.

You don't see as much as you think you do.
You're not the only one who feels shut out.
They see us as the same. Every bit of history they teach,
they might as well say: You can look, but nothing
belongs to you. They treat us like guests,
but look under our beds. Why were we asked here
if we were never meant to make this home?

Edmonia stares. Finally she says, But you're not like me.
You win prizes for spelling and Greek grammar.
Teach piano to the teachers' daughters.
No one ever accused you of anything,
even of not doing your homework.

Yes, I can play Mozart. But you're not the only girl
here who doesn't know her father.
My grandfather worked in a tavern to buy his three sons,
then one daughter, my Aunt Rebecca.
He never put down a dollar for my mother's freedom.

He *blamed her for* . . . Ruth chokes as if on a word
she can't say. It *was my aunt who saved*
the one hundred and twenty-five dollars *for me.*

New Year's Day, 1863

The old cannon in Tappan Square blasts.
Standing on the chapel steps, Mr. Langston
reads the Emancipation Proclamation:
   . . . *the people shall be then, thenceforward, and forever free.*

Students, teachers, and townspeople cheer, weep, shout,
Forever free! They beg him to read the words again,
then a third time, forgetting for a moment how the list
of slain soldiers on the church door grows longer,
forgetting the way won battles bring
not just triumph but sorrow.

A few weeks later, Ruth tells Edmonia, *President Lincoln's*
proclamation means colored men can enlist in Ohio soon,
but the governor of Massachusetts wants them to muster
for the Union Army now. Thomas is going to Boston to sign up!

You must be proud. And afraid.

He'd give his life for a chance to show the South
what's right and wrong. Ruth takes a deep breath.
I just worry whether he can pull a trigger.
I've never known a kinder man.

He'll have comrades, Edmonia says,
while you wait alone.

I'm not alone. But it's hard to wait to hear
how a story ends. And I'm sorry Thomas must interrupt
his education. I promised him I'd stick with mine.

Of course.

The mistress back in Virginia used to wear a new pair
of satin slippers for every ball, because we couldn't get out
all the scuff marks. One day I mean to buy
my Aunt Rebecca satin shoes for dancing.

When you're a teacher. Edmonia picks up a pitcher.
She cracks the thin coat of ice on top, pours a cup of water.

Ruth sips as if nothing could be sweeter,
as if she were thirstier than she knew.
She whispers, Thomas kissed me.
Did you ever know joy?

Broken Colors

Edmonia craves the smoky smell of drawing pencils,
like a burned-down fire, and hardening clay,
with its whiff of a pond bottom. She goes to the art room,
where each mark on paper offers a new chance.
She has nothing left but hunger for beauty,
small as the tip of a paintbrush.

She wishes the stove were lit,
though if smoke rose she might not be alone.
She smashes ice that sheathes
a jar of water to rinse a paintbrush.
She no longer draws goddesses, gods,
or anyone in transformation.
White people think metaphor belongs to them.

She opens a cupboard with boxes
printed with names, none hers.
She reads them as if studying a map
of places no one expects her ever to see.
The shelves and boxes are divided
like classrooms where walls come between
art, poetry, and myth. In history class,
teachers separate the dead from the living.
All through the school, lines are drawn between
right and wrong, white and colored, rich and poor,
truth and lies, fact and dreams, courage and fear,

what belongs to one person and what doesn't.
They forget that every time the wind blows,
the world asks everyone to bend.

She means to blend burnt sienna, carmine,
and Prussian blue. A cold breeze interrupts.
Mary Ellen and a girl she doesn't know come
through the door but stay by it.
The girl with straw-colored braids stares
at Edmonia and says, *Everybody told me about you.*
She bends her head to whisper to Mary Ellen,
then looks up and cries, *You took my paints!*

I *thought they were mine.*
Edmonia shuts the narrow box.

The Braided Rug

Father Keep's wooden desk is a fortress.
He and his wife fasten their gazes on pens
lined up like soldiers.

I *didn't take anything*. Edmonia never again wants
blocks of yellow ochre, cadmium blue, zinc white.
Look in my room! Look anywhere.

Not a single trustee believes you're a thief.
But we must consider the best interests of the school.
Father Keep stands, picks up a poker, shifts a log
that stirs the ashes. *We aren't telling you to go,*
but advising that you don't come back next semester.

Which is my last. Edmonia hears the tick
of a clock, its Roman numerals ringed with gold.

We hoped you'd make us proud. We gave you chances.
We know some folks in Boston, friends of your people.
Father Keep slips some books off a shelf. *Mrs. Child has written*
much about the evils of slavery and wrongs done to Indians.

As well as songs for children and "The American Frugal Housewife,"
Mrs. Keep says. *We expect she can use help around the house.*
Dear Lydia won't complain, but her husband often travels
and owes money she struggles to repay.

Father Keep says, *There's no disgrace in debt*
when money is lost to noble causes.

His wife opens a book and reads: *Shake carpets often,*
but spare the broom so carpets last.
Take in the clothesline every night, lest damp air wear it down.

Edmonia's broken breath is an effort,
instead of a simple exchange
between her lungs and the world's gift of air.

Naturally, we hope our students will do more than clean houses.
But these are hard times for everyone. You must think
of the greater good. Father Keep stares at the braided rug
as if it were a woven blanket spread before sightseers.
There's nothing left to sell and nothing saved.

The Empty Drawer

He wants you to be a maid! Ruth paces across
their room. Her dress rustles, crisp as broken patience.

*He didn't use that word. I'm to help around the house
in exchange for room and board. You always said
scrubbing floors is nothing to be ashamed of.*

*I clean to pay for classes so I'll never have to push
a mop again. They won't even let you stay
long enough to get a diploma?*

I need to go where no one knows what happened.
Edmonia looks out the window. She wishes she could
camouflage herself like a white hare on snow,
a brown toad by a tree trunk. She opens a drawer
and grabs her pencils like a fistful of arrows.
She packs her spare dress, her sewing basket,
a mended comb, a nightgown; she doesn't have much else.
She says, *I'll start again.*

*People can't choose where they start or stop.
Edmonia, we didn't have mamas who told us
we mattered, or pas who said:
You can do what anyone else can
or even what's never been done.*

But if two girls can be family, let me say
that I'm proud. You see more than most people.
You can change things with your hands.

Edmonia wonders if she'll ever again hear
another girl brush her hair, kneel on the floor,
set clasped hands on a coverlet for prayer,
breathe in a way that tells her she's included
in the entreaties. All she really wanted
was one friend. She says, *Come with me.*

You know I can't. This is the only chance
I'll ever have to go to school, at least one like this.
If something happens to Thomas,
I'll be all alone and must earn a living.

Maybe you'll see him in Boston.

Even if the regiment hasn't left Massachusetts yet,
a soldier can't leave the army
just because a girl wants to hold his hand.
I need to graduate. Teaching is the only way to rise.
You should teach, too.

You know I hate classrooms.

They must be different if you stand at the front.
Promise me you won't clean kitchens.

Don't tell me what to do. Edmonia can't say No
enough. She'll practice the word the way she memorizes
the rules of perspective. Her neck aches,
the way it had when waiting for the judge to speak.
I *have to disappear.* That's what could happen
to girls behind mops and brooms.

I *suppose this is a chance to leave the past behind you.*

My past is all people see. And it's not over.
They only admitted there wasn't proof to jail me.
I *have to show everyone I'm innocent.*

How *can you do that?*

I *don't know.* Or even remember exactly
what was said, who poured spices in the cider.
It *wasn't right that Hagar had to leave.*
She did nothing wrong. What happened to her?

Didn't *I tell you? She found a safe place.*

You're *lying.*

The good book doesn't say everything.
But Hagar made a new home.
She was in the desert,
but an angel brought her a cup of water.

Did she ever stop being angry?
Water wasn't enough.
Was she ever happy?

You will be, Edmonia.

No one knows. She runs her hand
over her hair, dark, curling like smoke.

The Train

At the depot, Ruth steps forward, arms
stretched out with a carpetbag.
Edmonia can't hear her words past the window,
pasted shut with ice and grime.
The train speeds ahead by fields and words
scattered like stones around tracks she can't see.
She left behind even that packed carpetbag,
afraid someone might accuse her of stealing
something she kept on her lap or behind her feet.
She carries only bread and water.

With all Ruth's talk about where she's going,
Edmonia never asked where she came from.
What was she was going to tell that day
she asked Edmonia to listen? What chance was missed?
The unspoken words fit like tight sleeves
Edmonia can't shrug off, even as she tells herself
they don't matter. She won't see Ruth again.

The locomotive shears past ancient stones,
hemlocks, swamp oaks, gooseberries, and milkweed.
Red birds fly to escape the shriek of skidding wheels.
Silently, she chants, Faster, *faster*,
wanting to move more swiftly than memory
or manitous who won't stay under branches, stones,
or skin, but shift shape or disappear like shadows.

She has only the future now, a place her aunts
knew was necessary but dangerous,
as they stitched a slow way forward with thin thread,
making blankets and baskets too small to be used.
No one can steam straight ahead like the train,
for time buckles. The past insists on a chase.
Will she ever again see her aunts hunching over baskets?
Reeds bend when they're damp, so her aunts lifted them
to their mouths, breathing in life. They held birchbark
over flames, just close enough for it to soften, then curved
it into small canoes they spread on blankets.
Tourists offered a few coins for swift
journeys to places where they'd never live.

The train rattles on, unsteady as cheers
that can turn in an instant to threats.
Edmonia's arms ache as if pulling back the string
of a bow with no arrow to shoot forward.
She won't look back through glass and smoke
to snowy woods where no boy will take her hand
in a promise or a lie. She won't ever again stand
before a judge with the power to put her behind bars.
She won't find herself alone in a dark field.
She won't be like her aunts being chased out of the forests
or her father going north in the night
or Hagar heading into the wilderness.

She means to leave behind everything but the sky.

No place is safe. Danger is everywhere.
She is the clatter and drum on train tracks,
certain she's going the wrong way
and that she can't turn back.

Boston,
Massachusetts
1863–1865

The Good House

Checkered curtains catch dust and sunlight,
keep the world from fading the tablecloth.
In the kitchen, Edmonia presses dough into a rough
circle, patches a tear, flutes the edges, wonders
if Mrs. Child scrubs the sink and sweeps floors
the way her aunts burned cedar branches
to keep their home safe. Could a row of jars
capturing currant jelly do the same?

Don't roll the pin more than three times
or the crust will turn coarse, Mrs. Child warns.
Before filling the pail for the pig,
salvage scraps good enough for the grease pot.
And make sure nothing's in the grease pot
that's fit for the table.

Edmonia slides three pies in the oven,
two for needy neighbors, feels a surge of heat
before shutting the iron door. She must
make a home here where every scrap
of wool is turned into mittens or muffs,
every fallen feather fixed into a duster.

No one must mention how the basement can flood.
The pump may break, the well go dry,
the oven explode. Rats nest in rags under the sink.

The spitting iron scorches a shirt.
A teacup cracks, and glue
scores a line through a painted rose.

Rules

Edmonia tosses dust and ashes in buckets
she tucks behind the kitchen door. Every day
she sweeps away signs that anyone was here.

Mrs. Child looks up from the suspenders
she knits for soldiers. *My back doesn't bend*
the way it did when I was young. I'm thankful
to have help, but now that you've been here a month,
I should point out that Mr. Child and I don't make
so much work that we can't spare you part of each day.
You'd be wise to earn something to put aside.
Girls your age think about little but weddings,
but every young lady should be prepared
to earn her own way. No one can tell what may happen.

I *know.* Memory traps and snares words
spoken over teacups, and warns
about the future she means to keep small,
like a stone in her hands.

I *married a respected lawyer, but he takes only*
virtuous clients, who often don't have a dime to pay him.
I'm grateful I can write books and spin rhymes. But
we were talking about you. Mrs. Child's knitting needles
clatter. *Perhaps you could teach girls and boys their ABCs.*

No one would trust me with their children.

Goodness, no one listens to old stories.
But perhaps you could work with dear Mrs. Bannister
who tends to the hair of distinguished colored women.
Her husband is quite an accomplished painter.

A colored man is an artist?
The girl Edmonia used to be catches
the scents of clay, plaster, and paint.

I believe he even makes a living at it, with the help
of his hardworking wife. A good Christian woman.
I might persuade her to take you on as an apprentice.

Maybe I could be a painter.

Mrs. Child clears her throat. Of course there should
be more than one colored artist, and why not women,
too, though I'm sure I'd be scolded for saying so.
But I'm afraid your future is uncertain enough.

Edmonia nods good-bye to the girl who mixed paints.
Back when I wove mats and beaded belts,
my aunts said I had clever hands and eyes.
In Oberlin, we stitched blue shirts for soldiers.

You *can* sew? Mrs. Child's face brightens.
It's a tragedy how many girls today are brought up
without learning how to use a needle.
I know ladies with dresses to repair.
It's important to be useful.
Your work needn't be glamorous. Useful rarely is.

The Art of Disappearance

Edmonia fetches clothes to be mended
from brick houses with little land between.
She carries baskets past ladies who are tight-belted,
buckled, buttoned, their necks straight below hats
burdened with flowers cut from cloth
and feathers taken from birds they can't name.
Boys toss balls. Girls run behind sticks and hoops.
Boston's curving streets aren't courtrooms.
Here Edmonia doesn't have to shove past staring,
but her story still follows her like a fox.

She returns to the parlor to stab a needle
through cloth, shorten sleeves, widen waistbands.
The bottoms of fashionably full gowns
take entire mornings to hem.
Memories won't lie still, but stun, startle, dart
like her hand moving up and down, as if casting
a spell to hide the girl who holds a needle,
to make a world small as her stitches,
the needle's brittle point
the blades of scissors
a wrist's soft skin
coiled red thread.

Stains

Edmonia sews while Mrs. Child writes recipes
for pickles and puddings, directions for crocheting
penwipers and purses, remedies for stomachaches:
Steep tea in boiling milk and sprinkle in nutmeg.
She narrates ways to clean spots on gloves,
vanquish bedbugs, raise bees and silkworms,
and keep girls from turning vain. How close
to invisible can a girl get before she disappears?

Mrs. Child writes a letter to the president, then wipes
the steel nib of her pen and looks at Edmonia.
God's war shouldn't make us forget other injustices.
My first book was a romance between
a white woman and a Pequot Indian. I was charmed
by Mr. Longfellow's poem about Hiawatha.
She takes a breath. I *heard your mother comes from*
people I've long admired. Can you tell me
about her and how you grew up?
She leans slightly forward
as Edmonia wishes she leaned toward Ruth,
back when Ruth asked her to listen.
Plain interest unlocks the cage inside,
but she doesn't know where to begin.

Mrs. Child takes up her pen again, using
her third-best stationery now. She nibbles pie

left from breakfast, seals and stacks envelopes.
She says, *I'm asking friends to send coins to a hardworking*
but needy widow. Remember there's always someone worse
off than you are. She offers a scrap of crust to the cat,
who earns room and board hunting mice.
I don't mean to pry, but is there anyone who waits
for your letters? Or prays for you?

Edmonia hears a train whistle,
an echo of wheels scraping tracks,
sees smoke and an iced-over window
between her and Ruth holding out her arms.
There's no one, she says. She won't pen a letter
until she's certain of her address and how to sign it.
Sincerely is not a word she uses. Neither is *Love.*

Small

Everything she left, the wisps of smoke curling
from the stove, stinging her eyes, the stench of ashes,
is beautiful. She couldn't see that the day
she asked Ruth to burn her old moccasins.
Could she disappear, like those deerskin shoes
or the canoes and bark houses her aunts shaped into toys
to barter to people who wanted a past
fit for children's eyes?

Delivery

Edmonia folds mended clothes into a wicker basket,
winds a shawl over her shoulders, and tugs on her mittens.
She walks past bookshops, taverns, walls plastered
with handbills for lost dogs or lectures on Nature and Faith.
Here trees grow in rows, not from seeds snagged
in the paws or tails of foxes, dropped by birds, swept by rain.
All were planted by human design, in a city
determined as she is to forget what came before.

A wrought iron fence corrals elm and beech trees
on the Common, where men scoop hot chestnuts
into paper cones. An organ grinder tosses peanuts to a monkey
wearing a red cap. Soldiers in blue jackets and trousers muster,
practicing marching in step, firing muskets,
swinging bayonets, and running like the devil.
A thin man with an empty sleeve pinned up
uses his one hand to hold out a Union Army cap for coins.
People say the veteran can feel the arm he lost.

She's glad to be outside, even if not in the woods.
Thoughts come from trees as much as books,
whirl into the shapes of clouds. She watches
strangers. Mouths can lie. Eyes can hide.
But she has learned to read backs.

She passes shops carved into slopes so she can look down
into windows displaying rows of currant cakes, gingerbread,
red-and-white peppermints, gloves, lace-edged parasols,
and rows of gold rings set with garnets and jade,
strings of pearls, looped like the sun's path. She climbs
a street of brick townhouses on Beacon Hill.
Not one dried leaf appears on potted geraniums behind sparkling
windows. Edmonia considers that a seamstress isn't a servant,
but she's not a guest either. She chooses the back steps.

A girl with skin the same shade of brown as hers
opens the door and takes the folded clothing.
She offers Edmonia a peek into the parlor that smells
of lemon balm and beeswax, stale tea, an antique rug.
She shows off what she dusted: the crystals on a chandelier,
leather-bound books, portraits of grim ancestors,
a white bust atop a shiny black piano.

Edmonia hurries out. The basket she brought,
now empty, feels heavy with the girl's pride
in what she'll never own, not even the shine she created.

Still

Sleet starts to fall as she heads down Joy Street,
where children choose cold over crowded homes.
Girls jump rope, rock rag dolls.
Boys shoot marbles, chase dogs.
A woman with a baby on her hip,
her dress loosely tied around her ankles
to keep it from blowing in a delirium of wind,
pulls snapping shirts off a clothesline.

A ball skids across the street.
Checking for horses and wagons,
Edmonia kicks it back. A boy catches the ball,
then throws it to a friend without a nod to her.

She tucks her chin, insists there's no need
for the ordinary life that can't be hers.
She climbs a hill past the old burying ground,
where slate stones are carved
with skulls, hourglasses, and angels.

A man touches her arm. Wings press her chest.
A beak nips her throat. She pulls away,
skids through a puddle, meaning to escape
Memory, who creeps through the dark,
but pounces in broad daylight, too.

Her breath turns choppy as a river under a cold wind.
She ducks under brown birds who dart and swoop
for broken bread in the shapes of small fists.
Sleet melts in their small footprints
and on the dark metal of a larger-than-life
figure with a high forehead. The statue
is shown in a coat and vest pulled over
a plump belly and breeches of an earlier era.
She's seen busts of famous men, but never a statue
of a whole person. Alone on a pedestal, he can't break.

She runs her palms over the cold
curves of his boot. She must forever be content
with metal and not skin. Tears are stronger
than her effort to hold them back. She can't
ever again gaze into the eyes of an uncaged deer or a boy.

But perhaps she was wrong to wish
for smallness. Memory can find her anywhere.

Chance

Edmonia carries in logs for the woodstove,
then tells Mrs. Child some of what she saw.

Ah, that statue of Benjamin Franklin? He was right:
"Energy and persistence conquer all things."
Though I think these days money could have been better
spent feeding the hungry than on decorations for a park.

Edmonia runs her hands over books she dusted
but never opened, framed tintypes of people
she doesn't know. *I want to learn to sculpt.*
Ruth had asked her not to wash dishes,
clothes, and floors that weren't hers. Does it matter
that this is an abolitionist's kitchen and scrub board
or that Mrs. Child sometimes works by her side?

My dear, no one expects you to be a seamstress
forever, but the war means sacrifices for all.
You of all people should know this is no time for beauty.

I've saved much of what I've earned sewing.

I don't complain about your thrift, but
you're not speaking of pennies. Mrs. Child's woolen dress
smells of pepper and cedar chips

used to keep away moths. *Paper and paints*
are dear enough. Stone and bronze cost a small fortune.

Grateful doesn't mean she can't be angry, too.
Patience doesn't mean she can't raise her voice.
Only fury is on her side, but its flutter and weight
make her bend her shoulders, duck.
She says, *You're right. Never mind.*

Mrs. Child looks up, as if she heard
the ruffle of feathers or snap of a beak.
She leans over a basket of kindling
and says, *My dear girl, I was told*
you were found in a field, badly, badly hurt.

Who told you? Edmonia catches her breath,
as if that could keep her from returning
to the snow. *I'm not like Hagar.*

I was thinking of women closer to home.
We hear terrible reports from the South,
such that made some Northerners understand
the need for the War of the Rebellion.

Edmonia turns her face.
Violence has an echo, a sharp sting.

Mrs. Child straightens her back. I suppose
if men insist on monuments, there's no reason
why women shouldn't make them. Harriet Hosmer,
a local girl, sailed to Rome to sculpt in marble.
I've never heard of a colored person sculpting,
but I know an artist who might take on a student
in exchange for some housekeeping. Will you fetch
my good stationery? Not the very best, but not the everyday:
That ivory-colored paper with a bit of heft.

In the Art Studio Building

Canvases painted with blue and golden-brown fish
are tacked to Mr. Brackett's walls. Edmonia hears
a piano and sliding footsteps from ballet students,
shouts from actors rehearsing in other rooms.
A few women paint, but all but one of the sculptors
she meets are white men, most too old
to serve in the army or wealthy enough to have choices.
They stop in to exchange trowels or copper wire,
linger to discuss news of recent battles and the draft.
Some seem perplexed that she's not in school,
though nod when she says, I'm finished.
They recall that's true of many girls also seventeen
who are at home doing cross-stich, playing piano,
arranging tea and scones or fairs to raise funds for hospitals.

She hauls buckets of water, sweeps up plaster dust,
cleans picks and knives, twists bits of wood
around wires for armatures to hold up clay.
Her work pays for the chance to watch
Mr. Brackett bend over clay the size and shape of a heart.
His hair, the color of snow, with some strands the shade
of winter-pale butter, falls forward.
His curved back looks concentrated as prayer.

She mixes earth and water, as if her hands were weather,
a storm that could bring together two worlds.

One day he offers a cast of a child's foot
and clay to mold into its likeness.
She kneads clay like bread, but unlike dough,
which needs a sort of breath to rise,
the air bubbles must be pressed out.
She rolls clay into coils and balls,
then struggles to shape precise slopes.
The clay is too thick, then too thin,
the sole's terrain too wide.
Doubt knocks her elbow.
She holds back words: I *can't do this.*
Memory moves through hands
she curls into fists, which are no use
to an artist. She starts again.

She breathes in the scent like the river
where she dug clay with her aunts
back when everyone's knees were brown.
Has she come home or has she been tricked
into a sense of safety? She stays alert for chance,
her hands open, eager to press the earthy scent
back into herself, though she stays cautious
as she would in any barter.
Can she make a life with few words,
with curves instead of straight lines?
Can she trust her own two palms
and ten fingers, even through mistakes?

Risk

Her legs and arms grow hard from carrying
firewood for the kiln, buckets of water,
and lifting and kneading mounds of clay.

She molds more clay into the shapes
of hands, feet, and faces.
When Mr. Brackett points out what's wrong,
her face heats like the kiln in the corner.
What if he's right?
She can't do this. She's no Michelangelo.

Art is as dangerous as memory,
which can dart, spring, or hide in clay,
ready to snag her skirt, clutch her hair,
thrust a coat over her eyes, like the men
who took night as masks,
forced darkness to their side.
No one answered her cries for help.
No words stopped the pounding and poking
of fists, fingers, and feet.
Her mouth can't hold the roar
knocking through her chest.
Her hand can't melt the shard of ice she clutches.
She throws the clay across the room.

Mr. Brackett says, *Pick it up. Start again.*

She scrapes up the clay, flattens it,
keeps working to find a way
to live under the sky that stays far away.

Profiles

Clay reminds her of how much can change.
She prods it out, pushes it in, forgets, remembers,
one motion as necessary as the other.

When Mr. Brackett approves of the feet and hands
she molds, she asks, *Can people earn a living at this?*

Few would call it a livelihood. I prefer to work
in the round, but pay my bills by using paint.
He glances at his sketch of a haddock. *Fishermen*
will pay for something to look at come winter.
And I'm glad I made the trip South to measure
John Brown's face before he was hanged
for trying to help slaves free themselves.
He takes a bust from a shelf of brave faces.
Small copies that sell for less might be popular.
I believe you're ready to try making a medallion.

Edmonia pinches and presses out the lines
of a face in clay slightly bigger than a silver dollar,
flat on one side. Mr. Brackett advises her to soften
the arch of the eyebrows, lines searing the forehead,
the set of his mouth. The likeness takes many tries.
When both are finally satisfied
with all the features of a face,
he shows her how to make a mold.

She sifts plaster powder between her fingers,
then swiftly stirs in water.
If the plaster is too thin, it won't harden.
If too thick, it won't take an impression.
She pours this into the mold she made,
tilting it to fill cracks, blowing so plaster seeps
into shallow hollows. When one layer hardens,
she warms oil and soap she paints on,
brushing away froth and foam.

After the disc hardens, she tips, taps, pries
out the fragile piece, prepares to make another.
Then another, taking and filling orders for her work.
Specks remain even after scrubbing, so each image
is slightly fainter than the one before. Like memory.

The Kitchen Garden

Mrs. Child isn't in the house, but Edmonia finds
her in the yard, tilting a watering can over witch hazel and sage.
She shoos away red and brown chickens and shouts,
My John Brown medallions were accepted
to sell at the soldiers' relief fair! Profits will go hospitals,
but money from any orders I take there will go to me.

Mrs. Child sets down the watering can.
That noble man's courage helped start the war.
And now his face will earn money for good men in need.
I hear you refused my friend's offer of clothes to mend.
Can you tell me why?

I'll earn more sculpting than I can with a needle.
Edmonia steps around the rhubarb's poisonous leaves.
I've begun work on a bust of Mr. Longfellow.

Not only a gentleman, but he bought freedom
for some slaves with income from his poems.
Mrs. Child bends to pull roots the color of rust.
Do you have a patron, a buyer?

Someone is interested.
I'm working on more military men, too.

Don't forget about bread and butter, or aim too high.
You're young. Art takes time.

May I have a sheet of paper and a stamp?

The Letter

Dear Ruth,

How is school?
Are you happy with your grades?
Did Thomas go to war?
Did he come back?
I have an address.

Your friend,
Edmonia

She won't write:
Did you ever buy dancing shoes for your aunt?
Do you ever think about me?

At the Soldiers' Fair

People rejoice over the victory in Gettysburg.
They purchase lace collars, copper spoons,
or lottery tickets for chances to win a grand piano,
a flock of Merino sheep, or a two-ton ox.
Ladies from Twelfth Baptist Church sway as they sing
about sorrow, swelling rivers, survival, and starting over.

Near tables of currant cakes, jars of peach preserves,
pickled muskmelon, and apple marmalade,
Edmonia displays her medallions.
She takes two dozen orders, stifles
a cheer for each new name on her tally.

Between Footsteps

A dark sky threatens rain over the Boston Common,
jammed sidewalks, and shops closed for the parade.
Edmonia elbows past people waving handkerchiefs or small flags.
Mothers, wives, sisters, daughters shout, *Forever free*.
Children straddle their fathers' shoulders. Crowds cheer
for a thousand men, many with rifles balanced
by their necks the colors of elm, maple, or pine bark.
Police on horseback keep watch for rioters.

Robert Gould Shaw leads his horse in front
of the 54th Massachusetts Infantry. He pulls the reins
before a platform bright with red, white, and blue bunting.
Colonel Shaw's mouth looks soft under his mustache.
He lifts blue eyes toward the gray sky, away from a balcony
where his mother, sisters, and the young woman he just
married stand with backs straight as the soldiers'.

Clouds thicken as he raises his sword,
narrows his eyes as if against light.
Edmonia follows his gaze. Angels or manitous,
clear as water or wind, beat their wings.
Briefly they touch almost every other soldier.
One grazes the colonel's shoulder,
then a man who looks like Thomas.
She hears the feathery thud of wings

under the beat and breath of drums, fifes, and horns.
Are the spirits choosing who will soon cross with them?

Colonel Shaw sheathes his sword, tugs the reins,
kicks his heels into the side of his horse.
With eyes fixed straight ahead,
men march toward the harbor. Some are former slaves,
and sons of slaves, and freedmen.

One could be her father. She's proud,
watching knees rise, steps matching steps,
often with imperfect timing,
which might be because they haven't practiced long
or from a hesitation to take orders.
She loves the missed steps most.

Midsummer

The gray cat laps cream.
Mrs. Child's hands are still
beside a creased newspaper.
She says, *Colonel Shaw and half*
the 54th Regiment were killed
while storming a fort in South Carolina.

Edmonia picks up the newspaper,
finds names only of officers.
What happened to Thomas?
Light shifts as if stolen by lifting wings,
a slant thin as the line between death and life.

Sometimes I wonder if it's worth it.
Mrs. Child then answers her own question.
Of course it's worth it.
We'll win this holy war
and heal our broken nation.
She stiffens her voice until it cracks.
But dear Robert, and hundreds of other brave men,
all with mothers, many with wives and children.

And girls who hoped to be those. Edmonia recalls
Ruth's hand curved in the shape of the apple
Thomas gave her.

When Mrs. Child looks hard at her,
Edmonia says, I *wasn't talking about myself.*

Why shouldn't you have such dreams?

Before and After Clay

Edmonia crosses streets where soldiers marched.
She faces the balcony Colonel Shaw faced,
recalls how straight he sat on his horse, looking
directly ahead, while spirits touched shoulders.

Filled with memory, she goes to the studio,
rolls clay into strips, then balls that she squeezes together.
She gouges out eyes, presses outward to make a nose,
intent on every contour. She folds in questions:
Was Thomas killed or hurt? Where is Ruth?

She sprinkles water to keep the clay pliable,
binds loss and lastingness,
sculpts not the wavering lines of the lips she saw,
but makes them firmer, the young man's cheeks flat
as if he always knew his fate. She presses in tales,
like how he'd refused his salary until the men
in his regiment were paid the same as white soldiers.
He wouldn't seek safety behind rows of men with muskets,
but led the soldiers aiming to destroy a Southern fort.

A shadow slants through the room. It's late.
Outside, lamplighters lift long sticks to the gas lamps.
She sits in silence until he speaks.

Questions

Art is made of questions and craft.
What she doesn't know shapes her work
along with the hope that someone believes
in her even if that girl can't see
what's under her hands.

Did Ruth get her letter?
It might never have been delivered.
Mail is uncertain in war time.
Is she still in school?
Or has she moved?

Quiet Hallways

A few women in the art studio building paint,
but Anne Whitney is the only one with plaster dust
often embedded in hands that are almost as white.
She invites Edmonia to join her at the Boston Athenæum.
Tall shelves of books and replicas of Roman gods
and Greek goddesses turn people quiet.

Edmonia has never seen sculptures this big,
or oil paintings, with much half-hidden in layers.
She prefers the way sculptures keep important lines
on the surface.
The women are rounded and smooth.
The men's muscles look strong.
Some statues have missing arms,
but no one reaches as if in need
or shows signs of bruises or boredom.

Edmonia admires them all, but Anne says,
We have enough men on pedestals and goddesses of love.
The courageous don't always wear crowns. Someday
I'd like to sculpt a beggar, and make her look beautiful.

People don't want statues of someone wondering
what to have for supper, Edmonia says.
They don't pay for flaws and secrets.

A *true artist can't think about commissions first,* Anne says.

Edmonia knows she means an artist such as herself
with a father who provides for her roof and food.

Small Flames
April 1865

Bells clang from chapels and meeting houses.
The Art Studio Building erupts with shouts:
The war is over! Mr. Brackett flings open his arms,
then drops them, shakes Edmonia's hand.
Drums and trumpets tap and blare
from the hall where actors practice.
Cannons boom from Boston Common.

As dusk falls, people set candles on windowsills.
Edmonia sets one small flame, too, in her bedroom.
Craving heat on her palms, she kneels to catch
dripping beeswax she sculpts into a gaunt face.

She continues in clay the next morning in the studio.
She carves shaggy hair, big ears, shadows
under the wide eyes of the man who buried his small son
and struggled to heal a split nation.

Days after news of General Lee's surrender,
Edmonia learns President Lincoln was shot.
Mourning moves through her hands.
Grief knows no borders.

But sometimes she feels glad
about the way there's no space between
her hands and clay, like sky touching earth.

Another Queen

In the line before the gallery, Edmonia listens
to people use the words *talent, genius,* and *peculiar.*
One lady says, *Miss Hosmer grew up near Boston,*
though now she makes her home in Rome. Her father
did his best after her mother passed over,
but the girl rode horses, paddled in the river,
was raised rather like a wild Indian.

The line moves on until Edmonia stands before a tall statue
of a woman who raises wrists bound in shackles
as if they were as light as ribbons. Zenobia's gaze
and gait look steady, even with chains around her ankles,
punished by Romans for her greed for land.
This is how her ancestor might also have been forced
to walk if she hadn't plucked an asp from a basket of figs.
Zenobia holds out her hands, even in shackles,
to show they couldn't take her spirit.

The marble's polish reflects light.
Smooth as teacups, there's no sign of human hands.

The Invitation

Harriet Hosmer enters the studio room where Edmonia works.
The sculptor's cropped curly hair is pushed under a cap.
A purple jacket is pulled over bloomers.
Her voice is brisk as she says, *My old neighbor spoke of you.*
Mrs. Child praised your ambition, but it was her comment
that you can get ahead of yourself that brought me here.
She turns to Edmonia's bust of Colonel Shaw.
It's popular enough that she's been taking orders.

This is better than I expected from someone
so young, Harriet Hosmer says.
Though I started young, too. No one could keep me in school.

I never saw a statue as tall as your Zenobia,
or as powerful.

I worked from a stone three times my height.
I was terrified it would break.

Why did you choose to sculpt a queen who became a slave?

Maybe she chose me. I escorted the statue here,
hoping for a sale. Then I'll go back to Rome,
where marble costs less, as it's cut from nearby mountains
and shipped down the river on barges.
In Italy, statues are our teachers. Come.

A sculptor must work in marble and make whole figures
to be great, though that's a word a lady isn't supposed to use.
I'll show you how to use hammer and chisel.
I could introduce you to a friend, a wealthy actress
who looks out for women artists. She'll give you a place to live.

Artists reveal. Artists hide.
Edmonia remembers a dream of going to Europe.
Can she swap clay the color of her hands for pale marble?
Carve entire bodies instead of life broken at the shoulders
and live where the ground is never hard and white?

The Gift

She makes one bust after another: seventeen,
forty-four, sixty-seven small faces of Colonel Robert Shaw.
She finishes one, collects money for another
to adorn mantelpieces in elegant parlors.
She likes molding clay, and setting those shapes in plaster,
but marble is smoother, with a sheen like pearls.
She calculates that the price of about a hundred will buy
her a ticket across the Atlantic, a train across Europe to Rome.
When she gets a commission for a bust of Abraham Lincoln
to be done in marble, she knows pine floors must be swept,
chickens fed, and dried apple pies baked without her.

She packs the few things she owns, writes to tell Ruth
she is leaving. In the kitchen, Mrs. Child is making jelly
from plums a neighbor thought too small to save.

Study the classics, she says, *but don't forget
your Christian education.* She spreads newspaper
under clear jars, stirs the bubbling, warm fruit,
licks a deep red stain from her wrist.
*Perhaps you can wait until the currants come in.
There's little ill a good currant jelly can't cure.*

The harbor will still be open, not yet iced over,
but Edmonia won't wait for that or a reply from Ruth.
She must go while she has the money and an invitation.

Mrs. Child gives her a knitted pair of slippers.
Did I tell you how much sickness can be avoided
by putting on slippers every morning?

Edmonia folds them so they fit in her hands
like the small sculptures of deerskin
her mother made when she was a baby,
smooth as a swan's wings collapsing back
into her own feathered body.

Rome, Italy
1865-1875

City of Marble

Snow-colored stone marks horizons.
Edmonia disappears into her own shadow,
past a marble emperor on horseback,
Neptune wrangling an octopus,
and tortoises diving past water-spouting fish.
A perfectly still Venus crosses her arms
over her breasts. Stone cherubs cling
to lampposts, bearing long silence,
always on the verge of breaking.

She shouldn't have come. History opens and shifts
like the present in a city where churches and forts
are overgrown with moss and ivy.

Even aboard the ship and riding the train
through England, France, and Italy, she was certain
she was going the wrong way. Here in a city
where carved men are part goat,
a girl turns into a tree,
and churches hold tales of transformation,
Edmonia remembers how much she hates change.
Stones don't give second chances.
Even marble can break like a mirror,
leaving no trace of anyone's face.

Tin Cup

Men scoop roasted chestnuts into paper cones.
Edmonia is hungry, and shouldn't be late for dinner
at the palazzo where Harriet Hosmer's friend
has given her a room, but she crosses a bridge
where angels seem carved by wind.
She heads into a museum where marble saints
fill rooms and hallways. It's forbidden,
but she glides her hand over a surface smooth
as a lake with no wind. What harm can that do?
She stops at a display of ancient coins,
one sculpted with a profile of Cleopatra.

She leaves to walk across stone older than the forests
where her aunts sculpted small homes.
Stalls display small papal flags, cathedral-shaped
inkwells, and miniature Santa Bambinos for sale.
Slate-colored birds fly over the piazza.
Rows of monks in rough brown robes chant.
A beggar in a ragged dress stretches her arms.
Without words, she shows what she needs:
Food. Shelter. Kindness.
She holds out a cup like the one of water an angel
gave to Hagar, though this might be empty.

Under Chandeliers

Crystal and silver gleam on the cloth-covered table.
Miss Cushman, a Shakespearean actress, has invited
Harriet Hosmer and other sculptors for dinner.
She assures Edmonia of the freedom she'll find
in Rome, and asks about the nation after the war.

There's jubilation and grief, she replies. As before.

A war means more monuments and memorials, an artist says.
We heard they melt cannons to make bronze statues.

Bronze can't honor like smooth white marble, Harriet says.
Though it can stand up to New England winters.

Where in America did you come from? a woman asks.
Her fingernails look worn by stone. They're rimmed
with dried clay. Her silk gown and pearls
and gold around her throat and wrists glimmer.

Another artist asks, *Why did you leave?*

Glances between guests
suggest that stories crossed the sea before her.
Edmonia wants to loosen memory's tight sleeves.
She glances at a servant who doesn't glance back.
Miss Cushman told her that Sally could make

a proper cup of tea and tame the actress's hair.
The more she praised her loyalty,
the more Edmonia felt forced to see
Sally's dark skin and Miss Cushman's pride or guilt.

She signals Sally to clear the dishes, invites guests
to the parlor for cheesecake and cappuccino.
Potted palms lean over a glass case displaying historic swords,
pistols, and knives. She points out the dagger
she used playing Lady Macbeth in New York,
the vial that she mimed held poison
when performing as Romeo in London.

Edmonia won't join the games of charades
or cards under chandeliers. She won't stand
between the grand piano and the case of weapons
while others sing Home, Sweet Home.
The gold-framed mirrors and velvet drapes
are far from the Oberlin boarding house's braided rugs,
wooden chairs, plain walls, and narrow beds.
Or they're exactly the same. China teacups clatter.

The Studio

Under a high ceiling, Edmonia looks through
tall arched windows to a courtyard.
The door is bigger than some in barns.

I used to work here, and before that, Queen Victoria's
favorite artist did. As if she can see her worry, Harriet says,
Miss Cushman trusts you can pay back the rent.
You won't always be sculpting folderol for tabletops.
You need the courtyard so no one must haul marble
slabs up steps and finished statues back down.
This neighborhood is convenient for tourists to stop in.

People watch you sculpt? Edmonia remembers
her aunts weaving sweetgrass while strangers stared.

Those who wouldn't be caught spending money
on art back in America want a souvenir and to say:
We found this in Europe, and saw the artist at work.
Yes, some come to stare. I explain that my short hair
makes it easier to brush out plaster dust.
Dresses are dangerous when climbing ladders
to work on tall statues. They don't listen,
but they buy my art.
Your story might bring patrons, too.

It's not true.

Most gossip isn't. Harriet laughs.
Come. I'll show you where to buy marble.

At the Landing

By the brown river, men wedge and push
marble slabs off barges. Harriet explains
how to check for consistent color and signs
of soft spots where the stone could crack.

Edmonia examines a stone about the size of a campfire.
*I have orders for marble busts
of Colonel Shaw and one of President Lincoln.*

Who would you most like to sculpt?

I don't know.

Of course you know.

Heroes, friends, maybe even a queen.
Edmonia stoops beside stone
she might know only when it's broken,
splintering light, casting new shadows.
She can almost hear it breathe.

Dreams

Two cream-colored oxen pull the cart with the stones
Edmonia chose. She and Harriet walk behind,
passing houses the colors of lemons, melons, and grapes.
Sprites grin from stucco walls as if they grew there.
Small statues of Madonnas stand over doorways.

Wide doors and tall windows are open.
Boys roll shirtsleeves past their elbows.
Girls' bright skirts swing around ankles.
Young women with bare feet bathe children
under spouting dolphins and splashing gods.

In some windows of shops,
bolts of silk catch the light.
China dinnerware gleams like milk.
Gold, diamonds, emeralds, and pearls blink,
looped around marble cherubs or dangling
from the chubby stone hands of imps.
Edmonia touches her hair, imagining pearls
that might make strangers see her worth. Then
she looks up at a girl leaning on a windowsill,
drying her black hair. Maybe she's dreaming.

Edmonia doesn't miss the sounds of dormitory
doors opening and closing, gossip after dark,

the sparkle on bureaus, combing and pinning
someone else's hair, or a boy with green eyes.
But sometimes she misses being a girl.

The First Winter

Harriet and a few other artists sometimes stop in
to advise or demonstrate ways to wield mallets,
chisels, and points. Edmonia learns
to chip away what's softer than what remains.
She breaks marble and memory, practicing
the art of taking away, so people will see
only what she chooses to save. She hammers
out stillness, holding a life in mid-speech or stride,
like a deer between danger and trust.

Her mallet pounds a chisel, which strikes stone.
The sound is sharp, like icicles splitting in sun,
louder than a china teacup settling onto a plate,
or heavy footsteps across a cold field.

Every day, she makes her own snowfall
of white chips and dust.

The Sculptor of History

Why learn about people from the past
if there isn't a chance they move among the living?
Edmonia doesn't expect, or at least not entirely,
her arm to be tapped by someone invisible,
or a whisper to arrive as if from nowhere, or stone.
But there's more to the living than touches and words.
History is made of forgetting as much as remembering.

Through the next year, she keeps up a conversation
with the past, sculpting busts of abolitionists,
senators, and the flag-bearer of the 54th Regiment.
Some seek her busts of Colonel Robert Shaw.
Unlike a person, a sculpture holds only one expression,
which Edmonia considers changing. She remembers
Anne Whitney saying that even heroes have fears.
Can a sculptor show not just glory, but its costs?

She carves the brave soldier as if doubt
never crossed his face.

Hers

Edmonia has worked for a year and sold many busts,
when Harriet suggests she start on big statues.
I'll give you the names of workmen who will follow
your models and measurements to cut rough forms
of the marble. Critics who know little
claim that means the art isn't ours, but it's how most work.

Edmonia curls her palm around a mallet's smooth handle.
She can't afford to pay for help, and
won't risk any hint that the work isn't all hers.
She wants to feel every stroke,
leaving signs in the muscles of her arms,
claiming every triumph, even every mistake.

The Room

She makes enough money to move from the palazzo
into a room with one small bed.
There's no carpet to sweep or shake, no sink to scrub.
She has a woodstove to warm coffee, but no oven
to scent the day with pie and procrastination.

No rumors or truths are laid like silver on a table.
There's just enough space to set her trunk
under the one window. There she keeps her clothes,
some tools, the wool slippers from Mrs. Child
she never took out from the brown folded paper.

Her strong, sore arm is a pillow as she falls asleep
to the sound of metal on stone. The beat won't leave
her ears at dusk, but blends with rain tapping
on windows, gushing through gutters,
teasing out scents from the lemon tree
by the door.

Hunger

The smell of fresh rolls, hot chestnuts, rosemary,
and sausages makes her belly feel bare as winter.
At the marketplace, Edmonia pretends
to study the color of apples, the shapes of oranges,
while calculating what she can afford. She knows
how many coins are in her purse and doesn't know
when she may fill it again. Empty is empty.

Was it a mistake to move from a place where breakfasts
and dinners were gifts? She returns home with one orange
she peels at the old table. She sips water, pushes back bills,
finds fresh paper and ink. On the worm-eaten wood,
she pens another plea. Borrowing makes her teeth ache,
but she needs money for marble to sculpt and sell.

Does Mrs. Child know of a park
or meetinghouse in need of another hero?

Splitting

Her hands shape stone,
which shapes the story she means to tell
with whatever the stone knew all along.
Reaching its inner planes, she listens
for a shift of sound that may warn of a weak spot.

She stays alert for the slight changes
in how her chisel enters.
One slip of her hand, a lapse of attention,
can make the rock startle apart,
fracture weeks of work into a maze.

A stone can break
like mirrors or history.
She can't ever look away.

Tightrope

When she hears a call from the doorway
—*E permeso?*—Edmonia steps out of the dust
that clouds her eyes, leaves grit under her teeth,
between her fingers, behind her ears, tangled in her hair.
She greets a couple dressed in fine clothing,
then stands as still as the art they circle.
Some want mementos of honorable men.
Others prefer sprites and imps
with no message but foolishness or joy.

They glance from the small statues to her,
looking for tales to take home.
Some faces flicker with surprise and efforts to hide it.
Some spill praise. Others offer advice,
or say, *She's young. True art takes time.*

Edmonia straightens to keep her balance
between presumption's batter and swing.

A Way Back

Months have different names, but through the times
of Snow Crust, Broken Snowshoes, then Maple-Sugar-Making,
Edmonia hunches over her work the way her aunts had
over baskets woven of rumor, nostalgia, and some truth.
One afternoon, a wealthy widow with two homes
to decorate orders a marble statue of Minnehaha
bidding her father good-bye.

Edmonia's hands smell like a riverbank
as she rehearses expressions in soft, changeable clay,
which soothes her palms.

Then holding the vision of a face, she steps
toward a great block of marble. She swings a mallet
onto a thick, pointed chisel. She cuts away coarse layers
toward imagination's strong, sure lines.
Slowly she sees a Sioux man carving arrowheads
just before his daughter leaves everything
she knows to live among the Ojibwe.

Two figures in one stone double the risks.
But she loves the heft of the chisel,
the scent and taste on her tongue of soft warm dust,
the sting as small chips bounce off her skin,
the clamor she creates. As a face's features emerge,
it takes more effort to tap more gently. She knows

she's near the end when her breath flows
smoothly as a needle through deerskin.

Leaving the studio, she's caught
between places and times.
She feels the curves of cobblestones under her soles,
the precise angle of air against her palms.
Briefly she becomes a girl in soft moccasins
again: Earth speaks back.

Forever Free

She knows what Mrs. Child would say:
She would be wise to wait for a commission
before ordering marble bigger than herself.
But Edmonia didn't cross the sea
to make art that fits on a table.

Memory curls like fists
as she carves sturdy shoulders
and hands clenched like Ruth's
as she prayed into darkness.
She smooths the girl's hair,
chisels slimmer eyes, nose, mouth,
and face lifted to sky.
She carves a companion with his foot
on a ball with broken chain, fist raised,
dangling sundered shackles.

She sharpens her chisels on a grindstone.
Then, carving more than cutting,
she tilts and taps a clawed chisel,
as if drawing into and on the rock.
As she works her way back,
her tools leave scratches and pale stun marks.

After days of work, her blows become softer.
Shaping muscles, making each arm and hand

unique, she needs more patience than strength.
She switches to a lighter mallet and smaller chisels,
making short, even strokes toward her vision
in the center of the stone.

She can't risk an imprecise aim in twilight,
but hates to leave before night has fully come.
She rakes rubble to pile by the door,
to be hauled off by sledges. She lights candles.
Relying on touch, she pushes a rasp like an iron,
then rubs a rough stone over the girl's face.
She dips a cloth in a pail of water and wipes off dust.
Smooth marble catches her reflection,
there, then gone.

The Sculptor

Edmonia rises in the new light, hearing wagons clatter
as they carry pails of milk, blocks of ice cut
from the mountains, fresh fish, and crates of leafy greens.

On her way to her studio, she passes the Caffè Greco,
where men in berets and rumpled shirts drink espresso
at round tables and argue about the colors of shadows.
Girls wearing veils climb in two straight lines
up the Spanish Steps to the convent school.
At the bottom of the steps, models sell violets
or offer Italian lessons along with a pose.
Some women knit beside daughters costumed
as Mary Magdalene. Others bounce babies
on their laps, hoping artists will add wings
to turn them into cherubs.

Edmonia stops at a stall where girls who work in vineyards
buy bright skirts. A red one with a ruffled hem
will sway just above her ankles. She buys a crimson cap
and a black velvet jacket with sleeves split below
the elbow so she can swing her arms,
and cropped at the waist so it won't slow her stride.

Back in her room, she opens the blades
of her scissors, holds up her hair, and cuts

strand by strand. It curls just under her ears.
She won't try to pin it flat anymore, blend in.
She isn't a shadow. She wants to be seen.

The Letter

My Dear Girl,

Boston is proud, though don't let it go to your head.
Forever Free in the Twelfth Baptist Church is a fitting
tribute to the heroes from that congregation who enlisted
in the 54th Regiment, or mourn husbands, sons, or brothers
who sacrificed along with dear Robert. I'm sure funds
will be raised to pay for stone and shipping, though
don't most artists have money in hand before they purchase?

Be certain to watch your purse.
Of course you're not a girl anymore,
but doesn't everyone need advice? Remember,
if you cut your hand, to spread molasses over the wound.

Sincerely yours,
Mrs. Lydia Maria Child

The Dream

Edmonia unwraps the woolen slippers that still smell
faintly of pepper and cedar used to keep away moths.
She kneels by the bed, folds her hands the way Ruth did,
then hums songs about exodus and troubled waters.

She clasps the slippers as she sleeps and hears,
I *didn't mean to hurt them. Not anyone.*
They drank from cups they chose themselves.

I *know.* I *always knew.* Ruth hands
her a pair of soft, small moccasins.

Edmonia wakes, but not in the room where she heard
flames from the hearth Ruth tended
while washing blood from her dress.
Did Ruth keep the small moccasins,
burn something else, then put them
in the carpetbag Edmonia left behind?

She can almost smell the worn deerskin.
She knows the texture of each perfectly placed bead,
the deliberately ragged edge. Her mother
must have always wanted her to find beauty
in both careful stitches and unraveling borders.

Home

Edmonia shops from stalls selling toasted squash seeds,
fresh figs, caged chickens, stacks of blue and yellow flowers.
She buys bread, crusty on the outside and soft within,
creamy cheese, oranges so sweet they almost sting.
She feels tucked within the soft, bending walls
of a language she begins to understand.

A brown-eyed boy tosses a ball his friend fumbles,
but Edmonia catches and kicks back.
As it slams into the boy's hands,
he grins and calls, Il *scultore!*

A lock unclasps. The bars inside her break.
Can this city be a home? A story still follows her,
but it's less like a fox, more like one of the cats
that skulk among ivy and stone relics.

Night

Under chandeliers at the palazzo, the American-born
sculptors complain, argue, and exchange advice.
One woman carves profiles on cameos for exquisite pins,
but most make work people must walk around.
They discuss what to submit to juries for a grand fair
to celebrate their old country's hundredth birthday.
The World's Fair will display triumphs of science and art.

Who do you most want to sculpt? Harriet asks
again. Silently, Edmonia wonders if she can afford
to make something magnificent enough
to be chosen for this international show,
work meant to stand under a very high roof.

Soon she says *Buona notte*, starts walking home.
Candles in windows flicker over stone monsters,
angels, and ghouls carved around doors. A soft wind
shifts petticoats, shirts, and stockings on clotheslines.

A man reaches for her arm,
twists her wrist to speak close to her ear.
She pulls out of his grip and runs.

Memory remains a dangerous animal,
clutching her hair like the men who pulled
her to the frozen ground.

Back in her room, pieces of the past turn still,
but the weight of all that is untold plummets.

She's safe now, but failure is never far away.
She rubs oil into the cracked skin
of her hands, nicked by tools gone amiss.
She thinks about quitting cutting stone,
bringing back the dead, but what would she do?

She promised Ruth she wouldn't scrub floors
or pour tea and pretend sympathy for pay.
Besides, the women she sees buying fruit and fish,
pinning wash on lines, work with an ease
that shows they bring the baskets to their own kitchens.
They don't hire help. If Edmonia can't sell what she sculpts,
she'll have to go back and be told she expected too much.

No. She expects what she needs, what she deserves.
Come morning, she returns to her studio.
She makes marble split and spit.
Chips and dust fly.
She breaks what's before her
to make something beautiful.
With each swing of her arm,
she turns the room where she stands into home.

The Necklace

After work, she stops at a shop where gold and gems
shimmer in the windows. Just recently
she worried that she'd have to leave Rome. She needs
to save for stone, to make a piece, maybe two,
to submit to the World's Fair jury. But she wants
not only to win a place for her work, but something
to wear to the galleries in Philadelphia besides
her crimson cap, her old jacket, and bright peasant skirt.
She buys a string of pearls.

Then she walks to a cathedral. It's time to kneel and give thanks
for her long stride, sharp eyes, and strong hands.
Day after day, her tools cut stone and whatever comes
between pride and boasting, between the words for confidence
given to men and the words women are called.
She's glad for an art that doesn't deal in lines,
but blurs past and present, doubt and brave hope.

In the long shadow cast by a stone steeple,
a beggar in a torn dress and bare feet
stretches her arms, holds out a cup.

Edmonia stops walking. She unclasps
her necklace. Sunlight teases out
soft shades of blue, pink, and yellow
she pours into the tin cup.

Pearls coil and clatter among a few coins.
A smile splits the beggar's face like breaking ice.
The woman turns back into a girl.

It's a gift, Edmonia says in two languages,
though she doesn't need to. She knows
whose beauty she must look for now.
For years she's sculpted faces other people might want,
and missed the girl who wants to be seen.

Stone Mirrors

Edmonia raises her arms to sculpt the body of a girl
she can't see but must find through her hands.
She aims a chisel, taps a mallet,
cuts a narrow path until she feels breath
on her wrists: Imagination and stone collide.
She chips marble, memory, a plain shift
that falls just below the knees of a girl
who hardly dared ask for a cup of water.
Her clasped hands stretch out.
One leg is set before the other
as if striding, but in danger of falling.

Edmonia chisels around soft spots.
Pale gray dust settles into her knuckles,
clings to her red skirt and loose blouse.
She splits stone and lines
between the girl who reaches
and the artist who sculpts a girl
reaching past the truth
everyone refused to hear.

Smashing the lines between courage and fear,
Edmonia feels the strength of her shoulders.
Then her arms stiffen as Hagar's must have
when the old man lifted her dress.
She pauses. Each aim and blow can ruin

not just an edge, but everything.
Her hammer reminds her to stay afraid.

Opening a way into the shapes of arms and legs,
she calls a young woman back into view.
She murmurs, Help me, Help me,
speaking for a young woman forced
to lie with a man. Hagar speaks back
of what Edmonia knew in her body all along:
When Ruth spoke about Hagar,
when she scrubbed the blood-stained dress
and wrung Edmonia's leg to save her,
Ruth was telling her own story.
What happened to Hagar happened to Ruth.
Both carried fury into a new land.

Edmonia sculpts pleading eyes, a soft mouth.
She can't mend what was broken,
but smooths scars and bruises.
Memory at last takes her side.
She drops her mallet and point,
opens her arms the way she should have
when Ruth offered the story
of why she had to go forward,
why she couldn't go back.

We're not the same, she told Ruth.
She was wrong. In the stone mirror,
Edmonia finds Hagar and Ruth and herself.

Conversation with a Queen

Still, always, there's more she needs to hear.
As Edmonia sweeps rubble and grit,
she wonders who else will step through stone.

Years later, she orders a piece of a white mountain,
a chunk as large as her old bark home
or the bedroom she shared with Ruth.
She leans into the stone, the world,
carving out lines that curve like ripples on water.
Splinters sting her skin.
Stone rubs her hands raw.
Chips fall, like belief and doubt.

She leaves flaws to make Cleopatra look alive,
but she won't sculpt the snake.
Even a queen isn't safe from herself.
She wonders if Cleopatra really wore pearls in her hair.
Did she slip potions into drinks? Poison herself?
Where did these stories come from?
None were penned by the queen, but even if they were,
would they hold any more truth, which unrolls
like a rug, each spin clarifying and concealing?
Soldiers might keep track of swords and ships,
but the more the story belongs just to one, the more
it may shape-shift between tellers and listeners.

Edmonia changes the past as she circles
the rough sculpture to see another side.
Sculptor and stone keep up a conversation.
As she carves Cleopatra, the queen shapes her.
Edmonia hammers, saying *Don't*,
as she said to Helen and Christine
all those years ago, telling them to put down
the potion that no one knew was poison.
Stop. She always knew that word
and who said it, but now as she carves
a way forward, the truth is whole and her own.

Her mallet pounds. Her point slips.
She's angry and desperate for justice
for a girl who was told the past could be left behind.
The stone of the queen's shoulder splits.
The sculptor screams as she witnesses the ruin.

The Death of Cleopatra

Edmonia bolts the studio door.
For a while, breathing is her triumph.
Then she kneels in what she meant to save,
but couldn't, leaving prints in the dust and shattered stone.
Really, she only ruined part of an arm and a shoulder,
the chance for Cleopatra to sit straight on her throne.

Even stones give second chances.
She'll show the queen with her head tilted,
as she might have been when she was dead or dying.
She'll sculpt the asp, the small beast
that changed everything,
though Cleopatra still commands.

Edmonia won't hide what went wrong
but make it part of the whole.
Art is made from what disappears.

THE WORLD'S FAIR
Philadelphia, Pennsylvania
1876

Earth and Sky

The streets smell of sausages, cabbage, and coffee sold
from stands. Horses with small flags tucked in harnesses
pull carriages past Lady Liberty's long sculpted arm
holding a torch from the roof of a souvenir shop.
Tourists at the Centennial Exposition can ride a train speeding
eight miles an hour around two hundred and fifty buildings
filled with displays of ancient Egyptian mummies,
George Washington's coat and trousers,
Queen Victoria's embroidery,
a cape made from the fluff of a milkweed pod,
butter sculpted into a princess,
and the Declaration of Independence recast from candy.

Rain falls as Edmonia walks in her bright blouse and wide skirt.
Her unpinned hair ripples like a river catching wind.
She strides past bronze winged horses on the steps
of the Art Building, which holds sculptures and paintings
from all thirty-seven states, several western territories,
and twenty nations. Inside, gentlemen shake rain
from their top hats. Ladies shut umbrellas.
Their gowns rustle like dried leaves, snapping branches.

In the galleries, heads turn toward Edmonia,
whose bright bohemian clothes make it clear
she's the sculptor. Gentlemen congratulate her.
Ladies wearing hats heavy with silk roses gush.

Edmonia smiles at praise from people around the world,
but she's most joyful to be someone with nothing to hide.

A small girl with braids tied in tricolored ribbons
touches the feet of Hagar. Across the room,
people bend back to see Cleopatra's stone face.
They raise their chins the way Edmonia once looked up
at the judge at the trial. She's been told
that her masterpiece has been seen by millions,
including President Grant. And, she supposes, by liars,
truth-tellers, perhaps girls who once folded paper swans.

A woman points at Edmonia,
who straightens her back, bracing.
The woman bends to a child, maybe five,
who scrambles out from the tent of her arm.
Her skirt billows over her woolen stockings
as she darts around people.
Her mother calls, *Don't run! Come back.*

The girl halts in front of Edmonia,
looks up past her waist at her face, then at her statue.
She asks, Is *that lady hurt?*

Cleopatra? That happened a long time ago.
Hadn't it? Present and past collapse together,

one never far from another. She's safe
in this moment, though that can't last.

I *like her*. The girl peers up at the asp.
She shouldn't have listened to that snake.

She needed a friend, Edmonia says. *Just one.*

The little girl tucks her head, opens her arms.
She throws them around Edmonia,
whose hands fall onto the girl's shoulders.
For a moment nothing comes between them.
Then the girl turns and runs
back to her mother, back into the world.

Soon Edmonia leaves the building. Rain falls
into her hair as she walks on, looks back.
Her self fits perfectly within her skin,
the way moccasins mold to feet,
a river wends through land,
or a crow slices her shape through the sky.

Memory
1876–The Present

The Death of Cleopatra was shipped to a gallery
in Chicago, then put in storage. The colossal sculpture
was later brought to a deserted field, a cemetery
for racehorses, then a warehouse. For almost a century,
much of the sculptor's story was hidden, too,
dazzling, disappearing, and then showing up again,
like waves that froth, rise, then curl under the sea's surface.

After Edmonia Lewis left Philadelphia, she traveled,
then returned to Europe. Little else is known.
Did she ever go back to the forest, looking for her aunts?
Did she find love with a woman or man that lasted beyond
moments or days? We don't know if anyone ever brushed
marble dust from her hair or if she ever nestled her chin
in the neck of a friend's baby. No one knows what
she regretted, longed for, or truly made her proud.

Some of her sculptures are now in museums,
but much remains missing. Conversations fade
even as they're spoken. Still, how does something many
have seen vanish from sight? How does history
lose track of a woman famous in her day?

People forget, move, quarrel, break things, and die.
Pianos were sold, fireplaces blocked, mantelpieces taken down,

and houses destroyed to make way for new buildings.
Historians still search for a gravestone. Will someone ever look
through an attic and find a stone face they don't recognize
crammed among chipped teacups, boxes of skates,
mice-gnawed candles, emptied perfume bottles,
a pair of crutches covered with cobwebs, bent spectacles,
broken clocks, albums of pressed flowers, and spools
without thread someone couldn't bear to toss out?

Memory doesn't follow a straight line.
The past changes every time we look back.
What can be guessed from the shape of stone,
and peering through the open spaces in questions,
has to be enough. History is not only caught
in vaults or glass cases, but is what's shoved aside
or deliberately left out: The letter left within the pages
of a book, what was whispered over cake or soup.

What's discarded turns to treasure.
What we have is enough, or almost.
Questions. Beauty. Love.

Who Was Edmonia Lewis?

(Mary) Edmonia Lewis (c. 1844–1907) never spoke or wrote much about her past, and some of the stories that have come down through time are vague or contradictory. Other peoples' letters, diaries, and memoirs suggest places she stayed, but we can't know much about who she saw or what was said. I read biographies and speculation, studied sculptures, researched the towns, cities, woods, artistic communities, and politics of her time, and looked for what seemed hidden beneath recorded words, plaster, or stone.

The open questions about her life frustrate biographers, but seem suited to verse, a form that delights in solid furniture and bric-a-brac, but is also comfortable with mysteries and leaps through time. Relying on both facts and gaps in history, I imagined my way into a sense of what might have been, the way a sculptor of historical figures starts with givens but creates her own vision.

Very little is known about Edmonia Lewis's parents, whom she honored in her work. Later in life, she may have visited her brother, who seems to have settled near the Rocky Mountains, but it's considered unlikely that she ever again saw her aunts. What seems certain is that the pride and strength she gained during her childhood among the Ojibwe sustained her through enormous hardships. And through the years, she increasingly credited her father and her mixed heritage for gifts of courage and tenacity.

Oberlin included a preparatory school when Edmonia Lewis attended. We know almost nothing about the other students. My portraits of Helen, Christine, Seth, and Ruth are fictional, inspired by passed-along stories of events leading to the sparsely documented accusation and trial. Real artists mentioned in the book include Edward A. Brackett, Anne Whitney, and Harriet Hosmer. As I did with Edmonia Lewis, I created their thoughts and dialogue by developing my impressions from letters, nonfiction accounts, and artwork. Other characters based on real people include John Mercer Langston, a member of one of the earliest classes to enter Oberlin, one of the first colleges to be both interracial and coeducational. His distinguished career included tenure as president of Howard University and work in Congress. Lydia Maria Child was well known as an author and for her work for human rights. Colonel Robert Gould Shaw died while leading the 54th Regiment in an attack on Fort Wagner in South Carolina. Edmonia Lewis's sculpture of him is now in the Museum of African American History in Boston, Massachusetts.

I cite only some sculptures, and, in the interest of space, naturally omit events. I ended with the Centennial Exhibition, which marked the height of Edmonia Lewis's fame as a sculptor, partly because around that time the neoclassical style of sculpture she worked in began to wane in popularity. Her reputation was revived in the 1970s, when interest in art made by women and people of color deepened. The Smithsonian American Art Museum in Washington, D.C., currently owns nine sculptures, including *Hagar*, *The Death of Cleopatra*, and *The Old Arrow Maker and His Daughter*. More than thirty other sculptures are in private collections, as well as at the Metropolitan Museum of Art, the Art Institute of Chicago, Fogg Art Museum, Newark Museum, Detroit Institute of Arts, and Saint Louis Art Museum. Edmonia Lewis is memorialized at Oberlin College with a center named for her that is dedicated to freedom and justice for all.

Main Sources

Most of the books here contain information about Edmonia Lewis and her artwork. Please visit the author's website (jeannineatkins.com) to learn about other books used to research sculpture, Oberlin, Boston, Rome, and the lives of Ojibwe and African Americans in the nineteenth century.

Bearden, Romare and Harry Henderson. *A History of African-American Artists, From 1792 to the Present*. New York: Pantheon Books, 1993.

Buick, Kirsten Pai. *Child of the Fire: Mary Edmonia Lewis and the Problem of Art History's Black and Indian Subject*. Durham, NC, and London: Duke University Press, 2010.

Henderson, Harry and Albert Henderson. *The Indomitable Spirit of Edmonia Lewis*. Milford, CT: Esquiline Hill Press, 2013.

Johnston, Basil. *Ojibway Heritage*. Lincoln and London: University of Nebraska Press, 1976.

Langston, John Mercer. *From the Virginia Plantation to the National Capitol*. New York: Bergman Publishers, 1969.

ojibwe.net

Richardson, Marilyn. "Vita: Edmonia Lewis." *Harvard Magazine*, 1986.

Rubinstein, Charlotte Streifer. *American Women Sculptors*. Boston: G.K. Hall and Co., 1990.

Shuttlesworth, Carolyn (editor). *Three Generations of African American Women Sculptors: A Study in Paradox*. Philadelphia: Afro-American Historical and Cultural Museum, 1996.

Sterling, Dorothy (editor). *We Are Your Sisters: Black Women in the Nineteenth Century*. New York and London: W.W. Norton, 1985.

Vizenor, Gerald. *The People Named the Chippewa*. Minneapolis and London: University of Minnesota Press, 1984.

Wolfe, Rinna Evelyn. *Edmonia Lewis: Wildfire in Marble*. Parsippany, NJ: Dillon Press, 1998.